PLAY IT AGAIN PADDY

Drogheda: An Irish Town Steeped in Music

HARRY O'REILLY

PLAY IT AGAIN PADDY
Drogheda: An Irish Town Steeped in Music

Published by: Harry O'Reilly
Distributed by: Harry O'Reilly Publications
Email address: info@playitagainpaddy.com
Website: www.playitagainpaddy.com

ISBN No.   978-0-9572916-0-7 Hardback
                978-0-9572916-1-4 Paperback

The author has made every effort to trace copyright details but where this has not been possible and amendments are required, the publisher, will be pleased to make any necessary arrangements at the earliest opportunity.

Printed & Designed by Anglo Printers Ltd.
Locall 1890 624 624 | www.angloprinters.ie

The Toppers Showband:
Frankie Smith, Tommy Moonan, Harry O'Reilly (Author), Mickey Rooney, Paddy Toner, Johnny Milne, Tommy Leddy

CONTENTS

PREFACE

The information contained in this book was compiled through a combination of both my personal knowledge and experiences, coupled with my research of the period under review. My own involvement with dance bands only began in 1960 and as I entered what was an already thriving scene, I took the decision to begin the book with the bands of the 1940s. This decision enabled me to include some of the most successful outfits of the previous generation and this in turn provided me with the opportunity to introduce you to some of the great musicians of that era. Not only were most of them personal acquaintances of mine, but I was also very lucky to have the opportunity to play music with several of them before their retirement.

The book is mainly presented as a light hearted journey through the recent past, and as such, it is not a definitive account of all the bands and musicians of that era. However, I am aware that it contains quite a significant part of Drogheda's social history and it is to this end that I have taken great care to ensure the accuracy of the information contained herein.

It is my aim to provide a snapshot of how Drogheda's finest bands and musicians emerged from their humble beginnings and went on to achieve both national and international fame. Although this is quite a comprehensive account of the bands, groups and musicians/singers of that era, I found myself compelled by the sheer volume of the information gleaned to confine myself to the principle outfits of the day.

ACKNOWLEDGMENTS

During the course of my research, I was greeted by so many of my old friends and I must express my gratitude for the hospitality which was extended to me on every occasion. I am deeply indebted to all of those individuals who were so helpful in supplying me with the information and the photographs which I sought, and which were so necessary for the successful completion of this book. I must also thank my family, my wife Bernie, daughter Susan and sons Kenneth and John, whose patience and support was invaluable and without whom it would have been impossible to succeed.

A special mention is due to Noel Mullins, author and photographer (www.noelmullins.com) whose help and advice was invaluable to me in the compilation of this book.

~

DEDICATION

During the research for Play it again Paddy, I was saddened to realise how many of my old friends and acquaintances in the music business have regrettably passed away. I hope this book helps to keep their music alive and I dedicate it to their memory.

Tommy Leddy and Harry O'Reilly (author)
Photograph by John O'Reilly

Foreword
TOMMY LEDDY
The Sound Shop and the TLT Theatre, Drogheda

I've known Harry for well over 50 years. We first met when I played with the Toppers Showband at The Parish Night Show in St. Bridget's Hall Bothar Brugha, Drogheda and Harry was a solo accordionist starting out. He played a very nifty accordion.

Harry later took up playing the guitar and became one of the best guitarists in Drogheda. He joined the Toppers Showband and later the Chancellors Showband and for years we played all over the country. We shared top billing with all the best bands of that time.

When Harry told me he was writing a book on the dance bands and showbands of Drogheda, I knew it was going to be a winner. He always likes to do things right and this book is the first and most important book on the history of bands from Drogheda ever written.

We will enjoy the memory of the happiness we gave and the times we had. I'll be looking forward to your next one, Harry.

Tommy Leddy
The Sound Shop and the TLT Theatre,
Drogheda

Eamonn Campbell
Photograph by Peter Schittler

Foreword
EAMONN CAMPBELL
of the Dubliners

first met Harry in 1962 when we both played with the newly formed Checkmates Showband. At that stage Harry was an accomplished accordion player and yours truly was "trying" to play guitar. The Saturday evening before the band's first gig (somewhere in Mayo) he came to my house, 9 William Street, Drogheda to try to teach me Duane Eddy's "40 Miles of Bad Road"-he didn't have great success as we subsequently played it as a duet so that he could cover up my mistakes.

Little did I think on that Saturday night that 50 yrs on Harry would ask me to write a foreword to his wonderful book about the musicians of Drogheda and surrounding districts from the 1940s onward, or that I'd be mentioned in it.

I know, having read a few short extracts from it, that Harry has put a lot of time energy and effort into researching and meeting as many of the musicians and/or their families as possible (some of the photos from the 40s and 50s are amazing). He drove to Dublin to meet me and we spent about 3 hours in conversation, not to mention all the texts and emails that followed.

The book is a testament to Harry's sheer doggedness and resilience in coming up with the idea and sticking with it to its brilliant conclusion.

Definitely "A LABOUR of LOVE".

All My Best Wishes,
Eamonn

P.S. - I now know how to play that solo.

CHAPTER ONE

MY FIRST SHOWBAND GIG

I waited nervously for the arrival of the band wagon that would take me to my first gig with a dance band. It was on a Sunday afternoon in early June 1960, and I had not yet reached my 14th birthday. My mother was twice as nervous as I was, as she paced the floor whilst issuing me with a list of do's and don'ts etc. When the wagon eventually arrived, she approached the band manager, Ben Moonan, and proceeded to issue him with another list of instructions regarding my welfare, which included no drinking or swearing in front of me and ensuring my safety in getting to and from the gig. After receiving suitable assurances from Ben, I was allowed to take my place in the wagon.

The name of the band was The Silver Star Showband, and had been named after the Morning Star Pub in the village of Tullyallen just a few miles outside Drogheda. We were not entirely unprepared, as we had held a band rehearsal just a few days previously in a small country hall at Monleek near Tullyallen. The band name was not used for very long, because at that time, it was common practice with some outfits to occasionally change the name of the band in order to secure return bookings. (As you may have already guessed, we were not very good).

£2.10 shillings was my agreed payment for playing from 9pm until 2am at the venue in Menlough Village in County Galway. Incidentally, I recently visited this village to see if the old dance hall is still there, and although it is no longer used for that purpose, it is still in existence. On our way to the gig we travelled through Tullyallen to pick up a few more members of the band. When we called to collect our lead singer Gerry Saurin, his mother told us that he was unavailable as he had already left for Donegal to sing with another band. No doubt they must have paid him at least £1 more than our manager Ben had offered him. He obligingly left word to take his brother instead as his replacement, and so that night John Saurin came in his place (I should add here that 10 years later I married their sister, Bernie).

We travelled across the country in our band wagon, which in reality was merely a van which was otherwise used for transporting chickens. It was a 260 mile round trip, but luckily as it was during the month of June, at least the weather was pleasant. Unfortunately, when we arrived at the dance hall there was a power failure. This meant we had no microphones or P.A. system whatsoever. Apparently, power failures were a regular occurrence in that area, and the committee kept a large supply of candles on hand, which provided sufficient lighting for their dances to proceed.

I still have a vision of the committee members walking around the hall and holding aloft long-handled lighted candlesticks in order to provide light for the duration of the evening. As I didn't require amplification for my accordion I was nominated to provide all of the evening's entertainment.

In those days it was customary to provide a good supply of beverages for the visiting bands, and Brendan (Red) Goring took control of the distribution of same. And so, the rest of the band remained back stage drinking cases of beer and shouting words of encouragement to me. They roared "Go on Harry your F***ing great", and "give us another one", as they guzzled away.

I remember thinking that Ben Moonan's promises to my mother had been well and truly thrown out of the window. At least Red made sure that he provided me with plenty of the lemonade that nobody else seemed interested in.

We arrived home the following morning at 8.00 a.m. to find my mother standing at the door in a panic. My three sisters Mary, Irene and Gaye later told me that my mother had kept them up for most of the night praying for my safe return. This was just the start of many similar vigils for them.

Before I move on from this particular gig, I feel that I must mention a couple of things that I perceived about the occasion in general and which would remain with me throughout my playing career.

As we travelled through the villages and towns of the midlands and west of the country en route to our Galway destination, I experienced for the first time the very distinctive smell of the widespread burning of turf fires. On our arrival at the venue the second thing of note was the provision of a large pot of tea accompanied by a cold salad meal. This dish was prepared and presented by the well-meaning dance committee members.

From that day forward the smell of turf followed by the inevitable cold salad meal was guaranteed to spring to my mind at the mere mention of a cross-country gig.

CHAPTER TWO

THE BIRTH OF AN IDEA

Whenever two or more musicians are gathered together the conversation invariably turns to an exchange of yarns about their experiences of life on the road and no doubt I probably mentioned this one about Menlough on more than one occasion. Several years later, in the latter half of the 1960s, during one such encounter between me and two of my closest musician friends, Paddy Toner (drummer), and singer Mickey Rooney, the original idea for this book first came up for discussion. Paddy and Mickey rather forcefully suggested that, as they were extremely unlikely to ever get round to writing a book about this era, it was down to me to do the writing. As Paddy put it, "Harry, just tell them how it was back then, and, more importantly, let them know that we actually existed".

Many years have passed since that fateful encounter, but rest assured, now that I have finally come round to doing it, you will have the opportunity, not only to read about Paddy and Mickey but also, the many more local musicians whose names will appear throughout the course of this book.

I had no idea where this journey would take me, nor how time consuming it would be. I do hope you enjoy reading it as much as I enjoyed researching it, renewing old acquaintances, swapping stories, digging up old photographs, remembering those that are gone, and regrettably they are many.

Recalling Paddy's words, I dedicate this book to their memory, and if you happen to find yourself reading this then you are most welcome to join me. Hopefully you will find it entertaining, informative, and somewhat amusing, as we "Play it again Paddy".

I know that Paddy's intention was that I should just give an ordinary account of the music business. However, I found it impossible to avoid writing what is, to all intents and purposes, partly autobiographical and a very personal account.

My reason for expanding the scope of the book was to take account of our great musical tradition, and in particular to showcase the great musicians who entertained the citizens of my home town of Drogheda; to this end I have loosely divided the overall story into three parts.

The earlier section deals mainly with the hey-day of ballroom dancing from the early1940s through to the emergence of the showband phenomenon which occurred during the latter half of the 1950s. The focus will then move on to the decade of the 1960s which is generally regarded as the showband years. The third section will review some of those bands who continued to perform and prosper from the earlier decades, through to the post-showband era of the 1970s and beyond.

In addition, the third section will also contain a review of the individual musicians who continued to play with showbands post-1970, coupled with the careers of those who successfully made the transition from the showband scene and re-formed, very often under a different banner, to become part of the new and flourishing cabaret and lounge-bar music scene.

I have tried to avoid falling into the trap of ending up with a book resembling a telephone directory (merely containing a list of names and bands etc.). My overall aim is to produce a record of these talented individuals and to keep their memory alive and to this end I have included quite a large number of photographs, as an aid for the reader to "put faces to the names".

Finally, there will be an ongoing review throughout the book documenting the exploits and career high points of many of our very own home grown celebrities.

CHAPTER THREE

THE EARLY DAYS IN THE '50s

I'll begin by giving a brief account of my musical background, which began when I was just a child in the early 1950s. I had an accident and was taken under the wing of the local midwife, Mary Anne Smith, fondly referred to as "The Nurse". She lived four doors from my family home in Mell. I overstayed my welcome and spent most of my childhood in that household. Her daughter Maisie, and sons Peadar, Larry and Ramie, had all grown up, but were still living at home. They treated me like a little brother (or perhaps, a nuisance).

All the Smith Brothers played music and The Nurse's home was an "open house", where music was played and musicians came and went on an almost daily basis. Peadar was a GAA Star and played with the victorious 1957 Louth football team, and because of his associations in this sphere, the visitors very often included other sports personalities. Celebrities such as renowned musician and Louth football captain Dermot O'Brien, band leader Cyril Jolley, together with journalists and promoters, the Hand twins Mick & Jim were among the many visitors who regularly called to visit The Nurse's home. I will deal with this period in much more detail later on in the story.

First off, to set the scene for the book, I will begin by taking a brief look at Ireland during the war years of the 1940s.

Prior to the advent of World War Two dancing was quite a popular form of entertainment but it really came into its own in the post war years when it became the in-thing for the youth of those bleak days. There were of course cinemas everywhere but dance halls experienced an explosion in attendance numbers and dancing rapidly overtook all other recreational activities to become the number one pastime of choice.

There were several dance venues dotted around Drogheda such as The Mayorality rooms and the A.O.H. hall but The Whitworth Hall was undoubtedly the prime venue of the day. I suppose the dancing craze came about from seeing dance sessions and competitions on the American influenced films of

The Drogheda Musical Society 1938

Mary Black, A. Quinn, Mary O'Mahoney, Tony McMahon, Miss McCullough, Christy Leonard, Carmel Daly, Henry Rundle, E. Carolan, Addie O'Grady, Benny McDonnell, Lily Hegarty, George Ledingham, May Leech, Bill Reynolds. Sitting in front: Brian Cassidy

the time. The popularity of dancing was also instrumental in the formation of a number of local bands/orchestras.

I listened to my mother and father talking about the local stars who played in these venues, and of course, the Whitworth Hall usually received a very favourable mention. Dancing took place here on several occasions each week. The promoters often held dance competitions and the contestants were judged by professional dancers. The admission charges ranged from as low as 1s/6d (Sunday afternoons), to as high as £1.00.

My parents told me that they loved to spend some of their special evenings there and to this day I still have a vision of a grandiose place where the ordinary people could go and feel really special.

Meanwhile, there was a growing rivalry between the various local bands who wanted to perform at the Whitworth. But, in my view, it was this same rivalry that actually led to the creation of the best bands in the country. The demand for Drogheda bands to perform both locally and nationally grew immensely. For a while, they enjoyed a golden period.

Some of the bands were really great but as usual there were some not-so-great, some of whom, I must confess, I also played with early in my career. (I just thought I'd throw that comment in there before someone else gets to have a go at me). More about these later on.

Joe Hal Orchestra:
Pat Jackson, Bill Reynolds, John Donnelly, Anna Carton, Joe Halpenny
Back: Joe Leech & Tom FInglas

CHAPTER FOUR

THE ORCHESTRAS

As I mentioned earlier I will begin by introducing you to a small selection of the top Drogheda bands from the early 1940s through to the late 1950s. As I intend to deal mainly with the most popular bands of this era, then without doubt The Carlton Orchestra definitely fits the bill.

The Carlton evolved from a previous band of the 1930s, known as The Eddie Gargan Band and as I am dealing with the 1940s onward I will take up the story from there.

From the time of their re-naming The Carlton hit the ground running and through a combination of great musicians coupled with their enthusiasm for the game they were soon in demand throughout the entire country. The membership of The Carlton in the early 1940s consisted of Peter Donnelly, Brian Hoey, Joe Leech, Jimmy Fitzpatrick, Paddy White, and Willie Flynn. The band was never short on innovations, and when Ella Bannon became the band's lead singer The Carlton became one of the first bands to feature a female vocalist in its line-up. Ella was just seventeen years of age when she successfully auditioned for her role with the band and she was an immediate sensation. She continued as the band's lead vocalist for seven years, and during that time she was widely acclaimed and regarded as a national treasure.

As the band was a full time professional one, they performed continually throughout that period, and consequently, Ella required an understudy. This role was filled by another great vocalist called Joan Godfrey and when Ella decided to retire from the Carlton Joan was chosen as her successor.

In addition to her role as lead vocalist with The Carlton Orchestra, Ella also sang on several concerts with the famous Mountaineers Group, and in the latter half of the 1940s she accepted an offer to sing with The Silver Seven

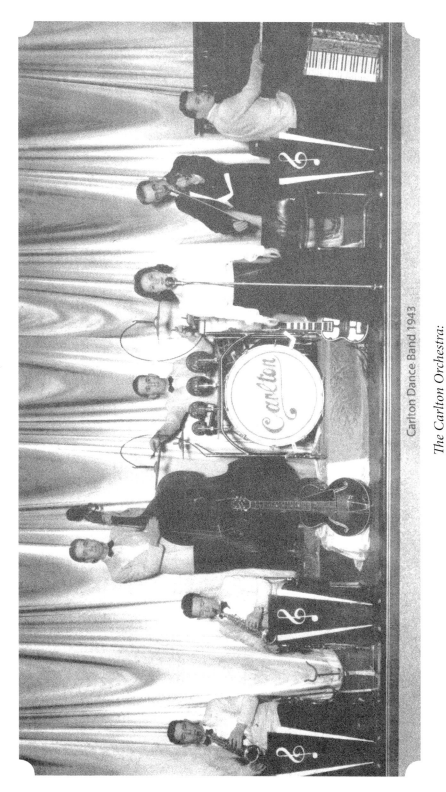

Carlton Dance Band 1943

The Carlton Orchestra:
Willie Flynn, Paddy White, Jimmy Fitzpatrick, Peter Donnelly, Ella (Bannon) O'Malley, Joe Leech, Brian Hoey.

Dance Band but her time with this outfit was rather short-lived and soon afterwards, at just 24 years of age, she brought the curtain down on her short but great career.

In early May 1948, The Carlton were booked to perform in the village known as Hospital in County Limerick, and when they decided to make the journey by air, they made their own little piece of history. It was most likely a publicity stunt, but it was carried off brilliantly and the press coverage that the event received further enhanced the band's already huge reputation. I should mention here,

Ella (Bannon) O'Malley

for the benefit of younger readers, the news of an Irish dance band using this form of transport in 1948 was, to say the least, quite sensational. They initially planned to charter a plane and fly to the dance venue from a field in Rathmullen outside of Drogheda, but as this operation was not feasible they took the more conventional route and travelled instead via an Aer Lingus flight from Dublin Airport to Shannon Airport. Either way, they did not miss the opportunity to exploit the situation for they subsequently renamed their band The Flying Carlton. They were accompanied by a group of friends and wellwishers to Dublin Airport, and when they arrived at Shannon Airport they were greeted by members of the dance committee. The venue was packed to capacity and the appreciative audience cheered the band throughout their mammoth performance which lasted from 11pm on Sunday night until 5am the following morning. Following their return to Drogheda it was business as usual as they prepared for just another routine gig in Mountnugent in Co.

*The Flying Carlton - Top: Joan Godfrey, Jimmy Fitzpatrick, Peter Donnelly,
Willie Flynn, Paddy Kearns, Tommy Matthews.
Bottom: Billy Shields, Paddy White, Jim Campbell, Terry Skelly, Annie Donnelly,
Paddy Kierans Snr., Sean Kerrigan*

Cavan.

The band had by this time undergone some personnel changes and the newly named Flying Carlton of 1948 consisted of Peter Donnelly, Billy Sheils, Paddy White, Willie Flynn, Paddy Kierans, Jimmy Fitzpatrick, and Joan Godfrey. As already mentioned, the role of lead vocalist was filled by Joan Godfrey, who had been recruited on a full time basis to fill the vacancy created by the departure of Ella Bannon. Joan, in turn, was equally successful and was widely acclaimed for her performances with The Flying Carlton. She remained with the band for several more years before deciding to call it a day.

They introduced yet another innovation when they acquired the services of Tommy Matthews, their very own full-time manager. Prior to his appointment, Tommy occasionally wrote letters regarding booking arrangements on the band's behalf, but was now employed on a more permanent footing.

The band also took their followers' enthusiasm to an even higher level when, during the late 1940s, they agreed to take part in the new concept of combining cinema entertainment with a live stage show. This particular pastime was referred to as Cine-Varieties, and took place at both The Gate Cinema and The Abbey Cinema in Drogheda. The Carlton Orchestra was the main attraction for The Abbey Cinema's version of these events. The concert environment provided the band with an excellent opportunity to showcase the individual talents of the band members and they put together a stage show comprised of solo performances from both vocalists and instrumentalists alike. By incorporating these performances into their dance routines, they were most likely an inspiration for what was later to become the showband phenomenon.

They acquired a huge following and went on to play at packed venues throughout Ireland, England and Scotland before finally calling it a day in 1960. The two line-ups indicated above were generally regarded as being the mainstay of the band. However, as the band was in existence for more than two decades, from time to time, and for various reasons, many other distinguished musicians graced the stage under the banner of The Flying Carlton. Included in their numbers were Willie Healy (trumpeter) and Johnny Barton (drummer), both of whom went on to become prominent members of several major local bands, Neil Kierans who later became leader of The Gresham Hotel Orchestra, Paddy Kierans (trumpeter),who also became a major band leader under the name of Paddy Kearns and played with several theatre orchestras in Dublin, Bobby Murphy (arranger and trumpeter) with the Radio Eireann Symphony Orchestra, and Jim (Jazz) Delaney (keyboards), who was also adept with many other musical instruments.

Furthermore, during the early 1950s, two of the band's original members, Peter Donnelly and Billy Sheilds exited The Flying Carlton and formed a new outfit which became known as The Flying Aces. I have included a separate report on this band elsewhere.

The Flying Carlton:
Jim Delaney, Paddy O'Connor, Peter Milne, Sean Cluskey, Syd Kierans, Joe Leech

When Willie Healy retired from the Flying Carlton during the mid-1950s he was replaced by Noel (Syd) Kierans, yet another member of The Kierans family, who is widely acknowledged by his peers as being amongst Ireland's finest trumpet players. Syd and I both shared a stage with Louis Smith's Delta Boys Showband during the mid-1960s, and Louis often featured Syd with some of his outstanding solo trumpet performances. In particular I recall his renditions of "Oh My Papa" and "Memories Of You", both of which were enthusiastically applauded by audiences everywhere.

Apart from the female singers already mentioned The Carlton also featured a succession of great male singers and included amongst their numbers were Matt Kelly, Ralph Lynch, and Tommy McDonnell.

The curtain finally came down on the Flying Carlton, when in 1960 the management of the newly opened Abbey Ballroom proposed to introduce a

The Flying Carlton: Peter Donnelly, Willie Flynn, Joan Godfrey, Jimmy Fitzpatrick, Paddy Kearns, Tommy Mathews, Billy Shields

resident band which would be known as The Abbey Ballroom Orchestra.

Both The Flying Carlton and Louis Smith's Dance Band were considered for the position but the final outcome resulted in the formation of a new band which comprised the full membership of the former Flying Carlton augmented with some members of Louis Smith's Dance Band. The duration of the residency was rather short lived and the arrangement only lasted for a number of months before this band also decided to call it a day.

Although the band folded in 1960 many of the members continued to display their talents elsewhere and their names will invariably turn up in the course of this book. I personally shared a stage with bands which at one time or another included former Carlton members Peter Donnelly, Syd Kierans, and Jazz Delaney.

Besides being an excellent musician Jimmy Fitzpatrick was also a master craftsman at making and repairing his own guitars and although I did not play in any bands with him, when the neck of my favourite guitar was accidentally broken in half, Jimmy came to the rescue and did an excellent repair job on it. Although this happened many years ago the guitar still looks, and more importantly, plays as good as new.

Finally, before I conclude my study of The Flying Carlton I want to establish a very important link between two former members of the band and another outfit who went on to achieve phenomenal success in the course of their career. The two musicians concerned were Jimmy Fitzpatrick and Brian Hoey and the name of the outfit was of course "The Mountaineers". I have detailed a special report on this band.

Similarly, I will also give a special portrayal of several individuals and outfits to emerge from the local scene who went on to receive both national and international acclaim. But before I deal with that matter I have some other great bands to review.

CHAPTER FIVE

MORE LOCAL ORCHESTRAS OF THE 1940s & 50s

When referring to bands of this era it's fair to say that they didn't come much better than Pat Jackson and his orchestra and that the man himself had reached the very pinnacle of saxophone playing. I have spoken with several exponents of this instrument and they all agreed that Pat was in a league of his own. He learned his craft during his early years as a member of The Drogheda Brass and Reed Band and despite his subsequent success and the drain on his time and resources he regularly returned to The Band Rooms to help with the tuition of the new recruits.

Brian Cassidy, who is himself an accomplished sax player, spoke of the hair tingling on the back of his neck as he listened to Pat playing some of his show stopping solos. Whenever he played such tunes as Saxophobia or Saxema everyone in the audience, including the dancers, stood still to silently listen to his performance before breaking into tremendous cheers of appreciation.

Pat launched his first outfit under the banner of The Pat Jackson Orchestra in 1938 at The Eldorado Ballroom in Oldcastle, Co. Meath. The band's popularity grew rapidly and they were soon in demand nationwide. Pat's Orchestra became one of Ireland's most sought-after bands and their appearances were always guaranteed to attract a capacity audience. Their popularity continued throughout the 1940s and for much of the 1950s when the decision was taken to disband. During the late 1940s the band took a well earned break from their gruelling and relentless travelling routine when Pat accepted the offer of fulfilling the position of resident Gate Variety Orchestra at the Gate Cinema's version of Cine Varieties. As Pat and his band were at the height

Brian Cassidy: As a teenager

The Astoria Orchestra:
Danny Kierans, Sean Kierans, Ramie Smith, Pat Jackson,
Jack Cluskey (Double Bass), Bill Reynolds, Dessie McManus.

The Pat Jackson Orchestra:
Bill Reynolds, Pat Leech, Pat Jackson, John Donnelly, Lily Fagan, Jimmy English, Tom Finglas, Jack Reilly, Louis Smith

The Astoria Orchestra:
Sean Kierans, Ramie Smith, Ray Buckley, Larry Farrell, Danny Kierans,
Paddy Farrell (Drogheda)

The Astoria Orchestra:
Standing: Sean Kierans, Jack Cluskey
Sitting: Dessie McManus, Jervis Martin, Danny Kierans, Stephen McDonnell.

The Astoria Orchestra:
Larry Farrell, Danny Kierans, Ramie Smith,
(Contest winner), Sean Kierans, Bill Reynolds, Patsy Carton.

of their popularity dance promoters throughout the country were very often disappointed at being unable to secure the band's services during this period. The format for the Cine Varieties at both The Abbey and Gate cinemas was basically the same with the showing of a feature film followed by a variety show, and as I have already mentioned, the Abbey Cinema's version of Cine-Varieties usually featured stage performances by members of The Flying Carlton Orchestra. The Gate Cinema's version was quite a different production and on occasions included a full scale variety event featuring the cream of Ireland's show business personalities augmented by some International guests. The reason for the availability of so many top artistes was due to the travel restrictions imposed on them during and after the war years. In order to bolster the public's morale the Government of the day openly encouraged cinema managers to engage in the production of these stage shows. This arrangement not only helped to keep the artistes in employment but it also provided some wonderful and otherwise very expensive entertainment at very little cost to

The Astoria Orchestra:
Johnny Barton, Danny Kierans, Sean Kierans, Jack Cluskey,
Paddy (Hardship) McCann, Dominic McManus

audiences throughout the country.

It was on one of these Gate Cinema variety shows that an outfit known as Louis Smith and The Harmonaires made an appearance. They were an eight piece group of singers featuring Louis. They received rave reports and as Pat Jackson and his orchestra were providing the musical arrangements for the show, I suspect that this may have had something to do with Louis becoming a member of Pat's band shortly afterwards.

Incidentally, when I enquired from Mick McGowan of The Mountaineers fame if he knew anything about this group he told me that not only was he aware of them but that he had been a member of the eight piece outfit. He also told me that it was the Harmonaires who recorded the well known radio commercial, written by Louis for The Imco Dry Cleaning Company. Readers of a certain age may remember this radio jingle which was played almost daily on Radio Eireann for several years during the 1950s.

The line-up that was most representative of The Pat Jackson Orchestra

The Astoria Orchestra:
Danny Kierans, Sean Kierans, Jack Cluskey (Double Bass) Stephen McDonnell,
Brendan Munster, Dominic McManus.

during their heyday was as follows: Pat Jackson (alto sax), Bill Reynolds (tenor sax), Pat Leech (bass), John Donnelly (drums), Lily Fagan (vocalist), Jimmy English (violin), Tom Finglas (guitar/banjo), Jack Reilly (trumpet), and Louis Smith (piano).

Pat's Orchestra, like most other outfits, underwent various personnel changes during its lifetime; the photographs will provide the necessary names.

****

Sean Kierans had been a fan of bands such as The Flying Carlton and The Pat Jackson Orchestra, and fresh from his trumpet playing tuition with The Drogheda Brass and Reed Band, he decided to form his own band.

Although Sean has long been associated with his well known outfit called The Astoria Orchestra he told me that the original name for his band was Sean Kierans and The Georgians which he formed in the late 1940s.

The Adelphi Orchestra: Brendan Munster, Kevin Martin, Henry (Henny) Bannon, Brian Finglas (Double Bass), Jackie Rodgers (Drums), Jim Byrne (Singer), Mickey Munster, Anna Carton (Piano).

The Kay Martin Band: Francie Martin, Frank Quinn (Bass), Kevin Martin, Ita Flood, Jemser White, John Martin (Accordion), Anna Carton

The line-up of The Georgians consisted of Sean (trumpet), Frank Boyle (alto sax), Brian Cassidy (alto sax), Pat Leech (bass), Tony Walsh (piano), George Reilly (drums), and Maisie Moore (vocalist).

Following a relatively short career they disbanded and in the early 1950s, Sean set about forming The Astoria Orchestra. With an already recognised reputation as a band leader and having established numerous contacts at venues nationwide Sean and The Astoria were very soon a leading attraction throughout the country. The line-up of this new band consisted of

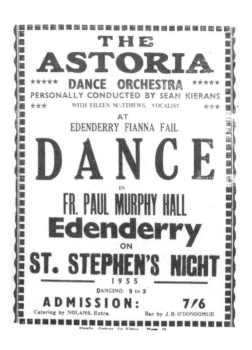

*The Astoria Dance Orchestra
1955 Poster*

Sean Kierans (trumpet), Danny Kierans (trombone), Brendan Munster (tenor sax), Stephen McDonnell (drums), Dominic McManus (piano), Jack Cluskey (bass), and Eileen Matthews (vocalist).

Having enjoyed a very successful run with this line-up during the first half of the 1950s Sean again set about re-organising his band for the remainder of the 1950s and beyond and to this end he embarked on a further change of personnel. Sean's decision to re-group at this time coincided with the disbandment of The Pat Jackson Orchestra and resulted in Sean's successful recruitment of both Pat Jackson and Bill Reynolds. The new look band consisted of Sean (trumpet), Danny Kierans (trombone), Bill Reynolds (tenor sax), Pat Jackson (alto sax), Ramie Smith (drums), Dessie McManus (piano), and Jack Cluskey (bass).

I recall sharing a stage with this line-up, when I was asked to make a guest appearance on stage with them in the late 50s.

The Stephen McCann Band:
Brendan Munster, Jack Cluskey, Paddy McCann, Mary Munster,
John Donnelly, Stephen McCann, Billy Shields.

The Silver Seven: Tommy McEvoy (Drums), Jimmy Corcoran (Alto Sax),
Jim (Jazz) Delaney (Keyboards), Terry Skelly (Trumpet), Martin Murphy (Tenor Sax), Benny
Connor (vocalist), (missing from the photograph is Paddy Connor, Dublin.) (Tenor Sax)

****

Brendan Munster, who played tenor sax with Sean's earlier version of his Astoria Orchestra, had previously been a founding member of The Adelphi Orchestra which was also one of the leading bands of the 1940s. Brendan together with his brother Michael (Mickey) Munster (accordion), headed up the Adelphi line-up, which also included Kevin Martin (alto sax), Henry (Henny) Bannon (trumpet), Brian Finglas (bass), Anna Carton (piano), Jackie Rogers (drums), and Jim Byrne (vocalist).

****

When Kevin Martin decided to exit The Adelphi and to form his own band he persuaded some of his former band mates to accompany him. This new outfit which was formed in late 1949 and continued until the mid-1950s became known as The Kay Martin Band. This band had a similar profile to that of The Adelphi and they played at many of the same venues. They were particularly popular at The Whitworth Hall where, during the early 1950s, they were booked to appear on a weekly basis.

The line-up which was most representative of The Kay Martin Band included Kevin (alto sax), Francie Martin (alto sax), John Martin (accordion), Anna Carton (piano), Jim (Jemser) White (drums), Frank Quinn (bass), and Ita Flood (vocalist).

Over the course of the next few years several other musicians joined The Kay Martin Band and included in their number were Jervis Martin (tenor sax), Jack Reilly (trumpet), Willie Healy (trumpet), Brian Finglas (bass), Mickey Munster (piano), and Jimmy Fitzpatrick (bass).

In the mid-1950s following an illustrious career, Kevin Martin decided to retire from the dance scene and to bring the curtain down on The Kay Martin Band. The remaining members of his band dispersed and many of them continued to play music with other well known bands of this era.

The Munster Family Accordion Band: 1936

****

During the latter half of the 1940s and throughout the 1950s, with the number of dance venues on the increase nationally, the demand for dance bands to perform at these new venues also grew accordingly and Drogheda certainly played its part in satisfying this demand. One of the main reasons why Drogheda was better placed than most other Irish towns to provide a seemingly endless supply of new dance bands was the wonderful musical training establishments which were already present in the town. I intend to address this matter later on.

****

The Stephen McCann Orchestra was another of the leading outfits to emerge during this period. The band was founded by Stephen with the help of his brother Paddy (Hardship) McCann. Although Stephen was primarily a violinist with his orchestra he was also adept at playing both trombone and mandolin. Stephen's musical career began as a young boy when his older brother Joe undertook to teach him how to play both the cello and the violin. Sometime later Stephen joined the Drogheda Brass and Reed Band where he learned to read music and to play the trombone. Stephen's brother Paddy was also a member of The Drogheda Brass and Reed Band during this period. The orchestra continued with its successful run until the latter half of the 1950s when the decision was taken to disband.

The line-up which was most representative of Stephen's Orchestra included Stephen McCann (violint), Paddy McCann, (sax and clarinet), Brendan Munster (saxophone), Jack Cluskey (double bass), John Donnelly (drums), Billy Sheils (piano/accordion), and Mary Munster (vocalist).

****

The Silver Seven Orchestra was founded during the early 1940s and their successful run continued right through to the latter half of the 1950s. Jimmy Corcoran (alto saxophone) was one of the founding members and he remained with the band throughout its existence. The Silver Seven was regularly featured at local venues such as The Whitworth Hall and they travelled extensively to gigs throughout the country. Like so many other bands from this period, due to the lengthy spell that they enjoyed, there were many changes in personnel. A representative line-up of The Silver Seven Orchestra during the 1950s consisted of Jimmy Corcoran (alto sax), Paddy Connor (tenor sax), Martin Murphy (tenor sax), Terry Skelly (trumpet), Jim (Jazz) Delaney (keyboards), Tommy McEvoy (Drums), and Benny Connor (vocalist).

CHAPTER SIX

THE TRANSITION

Throughout the latter half of the 1950s and into the early 1960s the makeup of dance bands and their audiences began to change quite significantly. This was due in no small part to the influence of Rock and Roll. The average age of both the audiences and the musicians dropped dramatically when compared to that of the previous generation. The next few years brought about a period of transition where the old style of music and dancing merged with the new and many of the previous generation of musicians either retired or embraced the new reality. The era of the showband had arrived.

There are a couple of interesting points to be made regarding the difference between the earlier generation of bands/orchestras and those of the emerging showband generation. The first, and most obvious one, is that the earlier band photographs show most of the members sitting behind their music stands whilst performing whereas the showband members are generally standing during their performances. The reason is quite simply that the earlier dance bands played from the musical orchestrations provided by the band leader whereas the showbands gradually phased out the use of sheet music and instead built up their musical programme by listening to records or tape recordings of songs. They then rehearsed the selected songs before including them in their repertoire.

The use of musical orchestrations made it much easier for the earlier band leaders to fill any vacancies that might arise without the need to hold prior rehearsals with the new recruits. The music sheets were numbered and the replacement musician was simply told which number to select. This gave rise to musicians referring to songs and musical pieces as "numbers" (the next number is called etc.). On the other hand, showbands found it difficult to

Peter Donnelly: Drummer

bring in any new recruit without a prior rehearsal and in fairness, some of the earliest showbands were somewhat less than brilliant as they attempted to blend the old style of music to that of the new.

Most of the earliest showband line-ups were comprised of musicians from the dance/orchestra era. The new generation of youthful guitarists with a good deal of guidance from the seasoned musicians following a lot of rehearsals, quickly found their feet and improved quite rapidly. However, in their eagerness to display their new found talent some of the more adventurous young musicians decided to go it alone and to form completely new showbands made up entirely of their own generation. Unfortunately they took quite a bit more time to find their feet. Nevertheless, most of them survived and went on to become top class outfits in their own right.

A typical showband line-up consisted of a rhythm section (drums and guitars), supported by a brass section, (trumpet, trombone, and saxophone) and usually fronted by a vocalist. Initially there were numerous musicians from the earlier orchestras and dance bands available to fill the brass and

Jack Reilly & The Adelphi Orchestra

percussion sections of the new showbands but the completion of the rhythm section proved much more troublesome. Although the arrival of Rock and Roll provided great music for dancers and musicians alike it also highlighted the distinct lack of guitarists to complete the showband line-ups. However, there was no shortage of budding guitarists amongst the youth of the day who were only too willing to fill these vacancies and despite their immaturity and lack of experience they soon found their feet. Following a period of "learning as you go" many of these guys went on to become amongst the most accomplished guitarists in the country.

****

In my earlier account of The Flying Carlton Orchestra I mentioned that two of the band's founding members, Peter Donnelly and Billy Sheilds, exited The Carlton during the early 1950s in order to create an entirely new dance band known as The Flying Aces. Together with Terry Skelly (trumpet), a personal friend of both musicians, the trio were affectionately referred to as The Three Musketeers. This was one of those bands which began during the earlier dance band era and not only survived the transition period of the late 1950s but embraced the arrival of the showband era and with a blend of youth and experience they continued to attract audiences throughout the 1950s right through to the mid-1960s.

The Flying Aces first took to the stage as a six piece outfit, and the line-up included Peter (drums), Billy (accordion/piano), Terry (trumpet), Brendan Munster (tenor sax), Paddy Heeney (tenor sax), and Benny Connor (vocalist). With a wealth of experience behind them, and having already built up a network of contacts at dance venues throughout the country during their Flying Carlton days, the band was quickly established as a leading attraction on the dance circuit.

The band continued with their six piece line-up for several years, but when vocalist Benny Connor decided on a move to Dublin in the latter half of the 1950s the decision was taken to become a seven piece outfit. Benny was replaced on vocals by Nan McCormack (nee Smith). Peter Campbell (vocals and double bass) completed the line-up.

In 1960, following a significant change in personnel, a second version of The Flying Aces was launched. The new line-up included the three founding members Peter, Billy and Terry, together with Paddy Black (vocalist), Barry Cluskey, (tenor sax), and Sean Byrne (tenor sax). There were several personnel changes over the next few years, with many of the new generation of musicians learning the ropes with the veterans of this long established outfit. Finally, after a long and illustrious run of success, the decision was taken to bring the curtain down on The Flying Aces in 1966.

Included amongst the numerous local musicians who performed under the banner of The Flying Aces were Tony (Bubbles) Healy (vocals and guitar), Pal McDonnell (vocals and bass guitar), Tommy McDonnell (vocals and guitar), and Tony Wynne (trumpet).

CHAPTER SEVEN

THE ADVENT OF THE SHOWBAND ERA

following the disbandment of his orchestra, and with the showband phenomenon really beginning to take hold, Stephen McCann decided to take to the stage again, this time with his own showband. He set about recruiting a number of musicians to accompany him in this venture and shortly afterwards he took to the stage again with his new outfit under the banner of The Broadway Showband.

With Stephen's already established list of contacts in the show business industry the band soon made their mark on the showband scene. The Broadway continued their successful run of engagements during the remainder of the 1950s and for the earlier part of the 1960s. When Stephen decided to retire from the scene, he brought the curtain down on The Broadway and on his showband days.

From time to time and for various reasons, quite a few musicians shared a stage with Stephen during his showband days and included in their numbers were Richard (Richie) Whearty (trumpet), Jim (Jazz) Delaney (saxophone/keyboards), Tony (Bubbles) Healy (guitar/vocals), Pal McDonnell (bass guitar), Tommy McDonnell (guitar/vocals), Paddy Toner (drums) and Mickey Rooney (vocals). With the emergence of several new bands during this period, when any outfit took the decision to disband, most if not all of the musicians who wished to continue were quickly re-employed.

Although Stephen's decision to retire meant the end of both his orchestra and showband days, throughout the remainder of the 1960s and 1970s, he still occasionally took to the stage to perform locally with both of his sons Tom and

Stephen Junior.

****

Another veteran musician from The Drogheda Brass and Reed Band, and who also played a prominent role in the orchestra/band scene of the 1940s and 1950s, was renowned trumpeter Jack Reilly. During the mid 1950s Jack was instrumental in the re-launch of The Adelphi Orchestra. However, during the latter half of the decade, following another change in personnel and with a new line-up which included a mixture of youth and experience, The Adelphi became known as the Adelphi Dance Band.

Jack used his already established contacts with ballroom promoters to secure most of the bookings for his new band and in 1961 he was offered a semi-resident position at St Bridget's Hall in Drogheda, where the band was subsequently featured on most Sunday nights for the remainder of that year.

One of The Adelphi's earliest line-ups consisted of Jack (trumpet), Frank Boyle (alto sax), Eugene (Gene) Brady (guitar), Sean Donnelly (guitar), Benny Smith (accordion), John (Twick) Donnelly (drums), and John Leonard (vocalist).

In 1962 the band underwent some changes in personnel and, following the departure of Dermot O'Brien and The Clubmen from their regular slot at The Boy's Club in Yellowbatter, Drogheda, the new look Adelphi took up the vacant position, where they continued to play for the remainder of that year.

The line-up for these gigs consisted of the three original members: Jack Reilly, Frank Boyle, and Benny Smith, augmented by John Brannigan (guitar), Joey Halpin (guitar), and Tommy (Bongo) Donnelly (drums). Some time afterwards, Jack decided to take things easy and following his retirement, the Adelphi was disbanded.

****

The Eldorado:
Patsy Floody, Patsy Dowd, John Leonard, Gene Brady,
Joe Fagan, unknown, Tom Sullivan.

The Eldorado Showband was one of the new outfits to emerge during the latter half of the 1950s, and the founding member was Patsy Floody from Mell in Drogheda. Although Patsy also managed some other outfits, he is probably best known for his leadership of The Eldorado. In addition to his guitar playing and vocals, he is also an excellent accordionist and he very often featured this instrument during the band's performances. The Eldorado Showband continued from the late 1950s through to the mid-1960s and there were several personnel changes during that period. The line-up which was most representative during the band's heyday was comprised of Patsy Floody (guitar/vocals), John Leonard (vocalist), Patsy Dowd (tenor sax.), Gene Brady (guitar), Tom Sullivan (accordion), and John (Twick) Donnelly (drums).

Cyril Jolley

CHAPTER EIGHT
MY EARLY INTRODUCTION TO MUSIC

As I have now reached the early 1960s, which as I have already mentioned at the beginning of this book, marked the start my career with showbands, I will avail of the opportunity to recount my own introduction to music which began when my mother enrolled me and my two older brothers, Jack and Paddy, into the Drogheda Brass and Reed Band in 1953.

We were placed under the tuition of Jimmy Nash who was, at that time, the band's musical director. As I was all of seven years of age, I still vividly remember my first evening at the Band Rooms in Georges Street. Following our formal enrolment, we were taken upstairs to meet the formidable Mr Nash. Jimmy was greatly respected and admired, not only by his fellow musicians in Drogheda, but also in music circles throughout the entire country.

In addition to his dedication to the tuition and promotion of music, his reputation as a strict disciplinarian, particularly amongst the young would-be musicians, was indeed formidable. Nevertheless, he also had a wicked sense of humour. On learning that I had just been recruited, and also being made aware of my young age, he called me up to introduce me to my fellow classmates. Although I had said that I would like to learn to play the trumpet, he said that all new members must first learn to play the big bass drum. He took me to the back of the class where the drum was situated, and asked me to hit it as hard as I possibly could. Of course I had no idea that it was all a set-up, and with all of my classmates looking on, I gave the drum a good hard bash. Jimmy leaped forward with his head in his hands and roared, "Oh my God, he's just burst our bass drum". The class erupted in laughter and, following my initial shock,

Harry O'Reilly
Author age 10

I realised that the joke was on me.

Try as he might, poor Jimmy was unsuccessful in turning me into a competent trumpet player, but he did succeed in passing on to me some of his great passion for music, and more importantly, he succeeded in teaching me how to read music quite adequately. Two years later, at the ripe old age of nine years, a series of events occurred which changed everything, resulting in my learning to play the accordion and helping to nurture my interest in music still further.

In the latter part of 1955, my two brothers persuaded my mother to buy them an accordion. She enrolled them in the local Crilly School of Music, but they soon got tired of the novelty and packed it in. My mother wanted to sell the accordion, but The Nurse Smith and I persuaded her to let me have a go.

It was around this time that Cyril Jolley, the accomplished accordionist and future band leader became yet another frequent visitor to her house in Mell, and The Nurse persuaded him to teach me how to play the accordion. I took to playing it like a duck to water. In a matter of months I was in demand to play on numerous Variety Shows. So began my adventure into the realms of show business. I learned quickly and I was soon playing on radio and in various talent contests.

I have a very vivid memory of Cyril's first visit to the Smiths' home in Mell. Peadar and Larry had met and befriended Cyril when he first came to work in Drogheda, and on learning that he played the accordion, they insisted on bringing him home to meet The Nurse.

Peadar's prowess, like so many other accordionists at that time, was rather limited - his repertoire consisted mainly of a few old Irish ballads and a few jigs and reels. On the other hand, the Smiths were unaware that Cyril was a classically trained accordionist who had not only competed in the London finals of the 1950 all England accordion championships, but had walked away with the coveted title of All-England champion in the under sixteen division. Peadar put on his accordion, took a seat by the fireside and launched into a rendition of The Old Bog Road. When he had finished playing, he offered his accordion to Cyril and asked him to play something nice for The Nurse. Cyril rather reluctantly agreed, but insisted on playing his own accordion which he collected from the boot of his car.

When he opened the accordion case, a gasp arose from the astonished audience at the sight of the magnificent instrument inside. When he put on his accordion, he received a number of requests to play some old ballads. Cyril apologised for not knowing any of the requested songs before launching into a fantastic rendition of The Poet and Peasant Overture. I remember the name of the musical piece, because it was a very long time afterwards before I was able to play it myself. Cyril continued to play classical music for the remainder of the evening, and although nobody knew any of the tunes, the audience was spellbound with his obvious talent.

Parish Night 1958:
Mal Caffrey, Sean Whearty, Joan (McEvoy) Hodgins, Brendan (Bunny) Tiernan,
Paddy (Podger) Reynolds, Charlie O'Brien, Harry O'Reilly (Author age 12),
Tommy Moonan, Tommy Leddy.

The Toppers Group 1958:
Tommy Leddy, Tommy Moonan, Mal Caffrey, Paddy (Podger) Reynolds

CHAPTER NINE

THE VARIETY TALENT SHOWS OF THE 1950s

Variety shows, which also featured talent competitions, were extremely popular at that time. They were a very useful springboard for singers and musicians to promote themselves and they provided a hub for many of the major bands that were to follow. During my career I took part in several of these contests, not only as a contestant myself, but also as a backing musician for other contestants. The sheer tension generated by these competitions not only provides terrific entertainment for the punters, but also actively encouraged audience participation in the shows.

Some element of controversy invariably arises during these competitions, and in order to set the scene, I will relate a couple of incidents which occurred during the final stages of two entirely unrelated talent contests. The first one involved me as a contestant, and several years later, the second one occurred when I was a member of the backing band, engaged to provide the musical accompaniment for the contestants.

The first incident took place during the final night of a competition called Parish Nights. This was one of the major talent competitions of the late 1950s/1960s and was run by the local clergy as a fundraiser for the church.

As I waited backstage to be introduced for my party piece, there was a terrible commotion in the auditorium. When I anxiously asked what was happening, all that was said was "It's the Nurse Smith". She had jumped up from her seat, and from the floor of the auditorium, in front of an audience of more than six hundred people, she openly challenged the M.C. about his bias in the competition. She obviously felt that I was not going to get a fair deal.

The Toppers Group:
Tommy Moonan, Podger Reynolds, Tommy Leddy, Mal Caffrey.

Well, following a debate from the floor to the stage, and in the interest of the continuation of the competition, she was escorted from the hall by the Parish Priest. I had to go out and perform to the best of my ability. I did my best, but I knew that all she really wanted was for me to be treated fairly. As usual, she did it her way. The competition ended with the success of a great singer called David Eager. The runners-up were The Toppers Showband and I was awarded 3rd place.

As will become clear later on, I actually joined The Toppers Showband. Coincidentally, in a recent Sky Television broadcast, recording the history of this band, Tommy Leddy, our future Manager and Bass Guitarist, actually mentions this particular Parish night show in his interview regarding the history of The Toppers Showband.

The venue of the second incident was a very popular and long established lounge bar on Trinity Street, Drogheda. We were the resident band and we played there on most weekends. The four man group consisted of Mickey

Rooney, Leo Larkin, Vinnie Byrne and me, and the nightly routine rarely changed. The clientele rarely changed either. They were quite clannish and were not particularly welcoming to any visiting strangers. Usually we would put on a show, and during the course of the evening, invite the audience to supply the names of some of their members to join us on stage. Just like the routine and the clientele, the suggested performers rarely changed either.

One night John, the owner of the establishment, in an effort to instil some extra excitement into the proceedings, asked us if we would support his idea of running a singing contest. He felt that this was a good way of rewarding his customers' loyalty, as he intended to put a substantial sum of money into the prize fund. Of course we agreed, and left it to him to take care of the necessary arrangements. He arranged for the competition heats to be run over several weekends, and to culminate in a grand finale of six contestants competing for just three cash prizes. He also arranged for the successful contestants to be chosen by popular audience vote.

Please bear in mind that John's intention, perhaps rather naively, was that the audience were most likely to vote for a local singer and that one, if not all, of the prize winners would be chosen from his regular customers. I think it's fair to say that the standard of the local talent was somewhat below top class, and, inevitably, a few above average singers from outside the area decided to exploit the situation and join the fray. They overcame the likelihood of defeat through a shortage of votes by flooding the place with their own supporters, who arrived by the bus load.

The visitors took first, second and third prize and the remaining three finalists, each of whom was local, were left empty handed. Poor John was distraught at the outcome and was somewhat apprehensive that the situation might turn nasty. He pleaded with us to come up with some sort of a resolution. We had to think fast, because his regular customers were quite obviously becoming agitated and angry about this unexpected turn of events. He immediately agreed to our suggestion that he should offer a monetary consolation prize to the defeated finalists. We watched him as he made his way through the packed and noisy throng towards one of the beaten finalists. As he leaned forward to commiserate with her to offer her the consolation prize, a terrible scream rang out above the noise, silencing the entire packed pub. The hushed crowd looked on as she leapt to her feet, threw the money on the floor and as she glowered in John's face she roared "Stick it up in your a**e".

Needless to say, that was the end of John's talent contests. However, as talent contests played such an important role in the entertainment business in general, and also because of their relevance to this book, I will undoubtedly refer to some more of them.

CHAPTER TEN

THE HOUSE IN MELL

As earlier promised, I will now return to the Smith family home in Mell. The Nurse's son Peadar not only played for his local football club The Oliver Plunkets, but as I have already mentioned, he competed at the highest level of inter-county football and performed admirably for the victorious Louth Football team in 1957.

For the record that Louth team beat Cork in the all-Ireland final by a score of 1 goal and 9 points to Cork's 1 goal and 7 points. Peadar was able to bring the most prestigious trophy in Irish sport (The Sam Maguire Cup) to his home

St Malachy's Ceile Band:
Cyril Jolley, Sean O'Brien, Brian Lynch, Dermot O'Brien,
Jimmy Walpole (double bass), Phyllis McKenny.

Cyril Jolley & Dermot O'Brien

in Mell for further festivities. Before I finish writing about Peader, I might add that I taught him a few chords on the guitar. He became quite proficient, and he managed to get himself lots of gigs with a group called the Mourne Men.

Meanwhile, his brother Raimie, who was drummer with The Brass & Reed Band, had been cutting out a career with some local bands, and their other brother Larry, who also played the French horn with The Brass and Reed Band, entertained visitors to the house with his accordion and harmonica playing. Dermot O'Brien, who later became a national and an internationally famous accordionist and singing star, was also Captain of the successful 1957 Louth football team.

During his early years, when Dermot was honing his musical skills, he regularly performed in the house in Mell and he spent many a musical night there. Prior to learning to play the accordion Dermot had earlier learned to play piano at the Convent of Mercy school in Ardee. During the early 1950s he joined forces with Cyril Jolley and they played music together with the St. Malachy's Ceili Band. He later joined the already established Vincent Lowe Trio as their new accordionist. It was around this time that The Nurse received a gift of a record player and one of the first records that I played on it was an early recording of Dermot with the Vincent Lowe trio.

On the other hand, Cyril Jolley had been trained by a German accordionist, and his accordion playing was not only brilliant,

Dermot O'Brien

but his style of playing contained both continental and classical influences. Dermot quickly learned these new techniques, and I believe that it was this collaboration with Cyril which helped him considerably to take his accordion playing skills to a much greater level, and as we all know, he went on to become, arguably, one of the worlds' greatest accordionists. I will write much more about both Dermot and Cyril when I report on the band scene of their era.

The Toppers:
Podger Reynolds, Tommy Moonan, Ken Donnelly, Mal Caffrey, Pat (Pal)McDonnell

CHAPTER ELEVEN

THE HAND TWINS

As I've previously mentioned, the Hand brothers, Michael (Mickser) and Jim, were among the many frequent visitors to Mell. As the brothers were identical twins, the Nurse like so many other people, was unable to tell them apart, so she insisted on referring to them as "The Micksers".

Mick began his career working locally as a journalist with The Drogheda Argus newspaper, but it wasn't too long before his talents were recognised. When he moved to Dublin, his career really took off and continued in an upward spiral. He rose through the ranks, working at The Irish News Agency, and continued his progression with appointments at The Dublin Evening News, The Sunday Review, and The Sunday Press. He reached the very pinnacle of his

Jim Hand with his uncle Frank

Michael (Mickser) Hand.

profession, and became a household name following his appointment in 1976 as editor of The Sunday Independent newspaper. Following his departure from this newspaper, he moved to The Sunday Tribune where he penned a variety of features including Down My Way. When Jim and Mickser were treated to a joint 50th birthday party in Scruffy Murphy's Pub, the event was attended by admirers from all walks of public life, and the attached photograph was taken on that occasion.

Jim went on to become one of the top entertainment managers in the country. He handled the careers of practically all of the major entertainers in Ireland, and the list of stars under his direction reads like a who's who in Irish entertainment. Included among these were The Dubliners & Ronnie Drew, The Furey Brothers & Davy Arthur, Dermot O'Brien and The Clubmen, Paddy Reilly, and Eurovision winner, Johnny Logan.

In addition to handling the affairs of these and many other Irish entertainers, Jim Hand was regarded as one of the leading promoters of international stars and was instrumental in bringing many of them to Ireland. Included amongst the acts that he introduced to this country were Tom Jones, The Tremeloes, Roy Orbison, The Move, Marmalade, Donovan, and Billy Connolly. Indeed, not only did he bring them to this country, but because of his love for his home town of Drogheda, he often took them on visits to his family home in Pearse Park.

Finally, I would like to refer to a little gem which I obtained during the

The Denver Showband:
Kevin O'Brien, Kenny Doyle, Dermot Finglas, Frankie Cudden, Tony Barrett,
Roy McCormack, Noel (Boots) Mooney

course of my research for this book. I listened to an excellent CD about the life and times of The Hand Twins as told by many of the aforementioned artistes. Other individuals also contributed, together with members of the extended Hand family and their friends. For those of you who may be interested, and enjoy a good laugh, this particular CD was featured on the Gerry Kelly programme on local radio station LMFM.

As I have just referred to LMFM perhaps this is an appropriate time to mention another stalwart of the local entertainment world, whose name is, of course, Dermot Finglas. As well as being an excellent DJ many people also remember Dermot for his appearances on the local music scene.

During the 1960s, he spent some time as vocalist with The Denver Showband. I'm sure there are many people who would like to commend him

The Hand Twins.

---

for his continued support and promotion of local talent on his radio shows.

Following the parish nights escapade, I was persuaded by a couple of entertainers, who were locally famous for their exploits in the Drogheda Pantomime (Tech Caffrey and Jimmy Fagan) to accompany them on another variety show. They persuaded me to go with them to Northern Ireland (Magherafelt) to take part in a parish fund raising show. The show went okay. But what I didn't know was that they were being paid appearance money for the show. I naively thought that all of the money was for charity. When they asked me to rejoin them in another show and, at first, I declined, they offered me 10 shillings. I think this little extra encouragement convinced me to go with them. Even at this early age, I learned a little lesson about how the grown up world operated.

CHAPTER TWELVE

THE ENTERTAINERS

It was around this time that I encountered a touring variety troupe called The Martin Show. They were led by a great all-round entertainer called Harry Martin and comprised members of his extended family. They performed throughout the country before they eventually decided to settle in Drogheda in 1963. A typical Martin Show contained various musical acts, successfully combined with numerous short drama pieces, and I'm sure that anyone who ever attended their shows would agree that they were an extremely talented group of individuals.

Before deciding to make Drogheda their home, they occasionally played at the old Savoy Cinema on Fair Street in Drogheda. On one such visit, yes you've probably guessed, they ran a talent competition and sought entrants through adverts in the local media. I, of course, duly sent in my application form.

The Heartbeats
Sean Donnelly, Phil Smith, John (Twick) Donnelly,
John Leonard, Jim (Jem) Woods.

Harry Martin

The competition was a tremendous success, and it drew very large audiences. The overall winners were a group of musicians called The Heartbeats, and their front man was a guy called John Leonard, I also think that I was the runner-up.

Regardless of the outcome of this competition, I feel that it was significant in creating a lasting friendship, between members of "The Show", and several of the participants in the contest, including myself.

Over the next few years, several groups/bands were formed from combinations which included members of The Martin Show and many of the participants in the competition.

This seems like the ideal place to report on the hugely successful career of Harry Martin, who emerged from being the star of The Martin Show, to become widely acknowledged as one of Ireland's leading entertainers. This also seems like an appropriate place to report on the subsequent careers of several of his extended family, through the various bands and groups which they were instrumental in forming.

Harry was destined for a lifetime in entertainment when, at just four years of age, he made his debut stage appearance on one of his parents' shows. Following many years of taking part in the show, Harry assumed the role of leader of the Martin Show. He continued to present the shows to audiences throughout the length and breadth of Ireland until 1963, when he and his extended family took the decision to curtail the extensive travelling and to make their home in Drogheda.

They continued for a short while to stage their shows at venues which were generally within easy reach of their newly established base. However, as the show contained a readymade band of musicians they decided to take advantage of their new situation and they began to accept bookings for dances in and

The Denver Showband:
Brendan Crean, Jimmy Watters, Harry Martin, Noel (Boots) Mooney, Kenny
Doyle, Marie (Martin) McCormack, Roy McCormack , Jim (Jazz) Delaney.

around the Drogheda area. As the demand for the band's performances grew, they found themselves with less time to dedicate to their stage productions, and sadly the Martin Shows were gradually phased out.

The first band to emerge from the show was simply called The Martin Family Showband, and it wasn't long before they assumed the name of The Martones.

The band consisted of Harry, Gerry Farrell, Roy McCormack, Kenny Doyle, and Larry Doyle, and they were later joined by Harry's sister Marie, who took over on drums and vocals.

In the latter half of 1964, they took the decision to join forces with another outfit called The Viceroys, and this eight piece combination became known as The Denver Showband.

The line-up of this band was Harry Martin, Marie McCormack (nee Martin), Roy McCormack, Kenny Doyle, Brendan Crean, Jimmy Watters, Noel (Boots) Mooney, and Jim (Jazz) Delaney. They enjoyed a very successful career before they took the decision to disband.

Harry Martin embarked on a new career as a solo artiste, and his sister Marie decided to call it a day. Shortly afterwards, The Denver Showband decided to

The Cotton Mill Boys
Harry Martin, Eamonn Flood, Alan Barton,
Charlie Arkins, Fergal Grimes

The Denver Showband:
Jim (Jazz) Delaney, Jimmy Watters, Brendan Crean, Harry Martin, Noel (Boots) Mooney,
Roy McCormack, Marie (Martin) McCormack, Kenny Doyle

reform as a six piece outfit and the new line-up consisted of Roy McCormack, Kenny Doyle, Noel Mooney, Frankie Cudden, Tony Barrett, Kevin O'Brien and Dermot Finglas.

Other musicians to perform with The Denver Showband included Clarrie Taylor, Robin Taylor and Terry Heeney.

Meanwhile, Harry Martin was enjoying life as a successful solo entertainer. His career received a huge boost when he was engaged as a headline act for Dan Lowrys cabaret lounge at Butlins Holiday Camp. He retained this position for several more years. His appearances at this venue also led to an abundance of cabaret engagements throughout the country.

In 1970 he was instrumental in the formation of a professional group of musicians called The Country Gents. This group consisted of four outstanding individuals namely Harry, (guitar/vocalist), Eamonn Campbell (lead guitar), John (Twick) Donnelly (drums) and Derek McCormack (bass guitar).

Their management affairs were handled by The Eamonn Andrews Studios in Dublin, and although this outfit only lasted for under two years, they enjoyed tremendous success during this period. They took the decision to disband and to pursue their hugely successful careers elsewhere, and no doubt I will be referring to each of them again during the course of this book. In the meantime I will continue with my review of Harry Martin's extensive career.

Following the demise of The Country Gents, Harry decided to return to the cabaret scene. He accepted an offer to perform as host and entertainer at Sharkey's cabaret and lounge bar in Clogherhead, Co. Louth. It wasn't long before Sharkey's became one of the east coast's leading venues, and this was due in no small part to the man himself. He continued in this position for a few years during the early 1970s.

Harry returned to the band circuit when he took up an offer to join the top country music outfit The Cotton Mill Boys. He was initially recruited to play with them for just a short period but he made such an impression that he remained with them for the best part of nine years.

This band was a major attraction and had a terrific following both at home and abroad. They travelled extensively, and undoubtedly one of their career highlights was their appearance at The Country Music Festival in Peterborough in England, where they received a tremendous reception from the assembled audience of 4,500 country music fans.

Harry also played with another outfit known as Spare Wheel. This group was comprised of several members of The Cotton Mill Boys.

Finally he decided to take things a little easier, and he returned to the less

The Martin Showband:
Jerry Farrell, Harry Martin, Roy McCormack, Chris (Martin) Doyle,
Marie (Martin) McCormack, Larry Doyle, Stanley McCormack.

The Viceroys:
Frankie Cudden, Tony Martin, Jimmy Watters,
Noel Mooney, Declan Reilly, Jim Walsh, Nicky Callan.

hectic lifestyle of performing at local venues, where he is still greeted with warm affection.

As I endeavour to maintain an element of continuity to this story, I will return later to review the subsequent success of several of the other members of The Martin Show, and the outfits in which they participated.

But I simply can't leave this section without writing about a little incident that was told to me recently concerning Harry Martin.

Now Harry is not only renowned for his musical talents and for his sense of humour, he is also admired for his longevity. Despite the fact that he is long past 21 years of age, he is still going strong on the entertainment front.

Well, the story goes that Harry and some of his mates were engaged to play at the millennium celebrations. On arriving at the venue, one of the boys asked Harry how much money had he charged for the gig. His reply was "I don't know yet, how much did we charge for the last millennium gig".

****

As I have already mentioned, the winning act on The Martin Show talent contest featured a performer called John Leonard, and following his departure from The Heartbeats, he also went on to enjoy a long and very successful career in show business.

Incidentally, The Nurse Smith was also famous for her home-made wines - elderberry, dandeloin, potato, you name it, she made wines from it. Everyone who paid a visit to her home in Mell was invited to a sample glass, and one of her biggest fans was none other than John Leonard.

Included among the various outfits that John featured in were The Eldorado Showband, Louis Smith's Delta boys and The Bee Vee Five. His name will most likely appear again in relation to these bands, as will the names of many of the other individuals involved.

In early 1965, following John's exit from The Bee Vee Five, he was invited to team up with Errol Sweeney and Dessie McManus as a replacement for Ralph Lynch, who had decided to move on. The new Trio adopted the name of The D Jays, and the line-up consisted of Errol (guitar), Dessie (keyboards) and John (drums). During his time with The Bee Vee Five, John had been taking drum lessons and had become quite proficient.

The D Jays remained together for the next few years, and most of their

The Country Gents:
Derek McCormack, John (Twick) Donnelly, Harry Martin, Eamonn Campbell

Drake Inn Finglas:
Dessie McManus, Johnny Ray, John Leonard, Errol Sweeney.

gigs were at The Village Hotel in Bettystown where they were retained as the Hotel's resident group. However, in 1968 the group's career prospects improved significantly when they successfully applied for the position as resident group at The Cappagh House Cabaret Rooms in Finglas in Dublin.

The country's top cabaret acts made regular appearances at this venue, and very often they required the musical support of the D Jays. Consequently the lads found themselves performing nightly in front of sell out audiences, and they in turn became a big hit with the punters. The news soon spread about the group, and after a while they were approached by the management of The Drake Inn Cabaret Lounge, also in Finglas. They were persuaded to make the move to "The Drake", and a large proportion of the audience from Cappagh House also made the move with them.

This move also led to what was probably the highlight of John's career, when he was persuaded to take over the role of singer and M.C. at The Drake, and his role as drummer was taken up by Errol's brother Ian Sweeney. The Drake began to engage some of the top international stars, and became undoubtedly the top cabaret spot, not only in Dublin, but most probably in all of Ireland.
I witnessed the spectacle of The Drake first hand, because as well as being the group's guitarist, Errol was also a top League of Ireland referee, and whenever he was required to referee important football matches, I filled the vacancy as guitarist with the group.

When Dessie McManus decided to exit the group, he was replaced by Drogheda musician Larry Carolan, and Larry was also later replaced by Dublin musician Eugene McCarthy. Finally, the group disbanded in the late 1970s.

As The Savoy Cinema/Martin Show talent contest was held during 1960, and as my debut on the dance band scene occurred during that same year, I will now take up the story from there with an account of my second gig. In addition, as no book on bands and musicians would be complete without including a few of the more amusing (yet still printable) stories therein, I intend to do just that. In hindsight some of the tales which now seem amusing, were probably not quite so funny at the time.

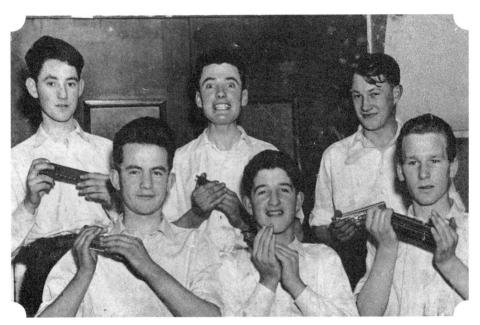

The Harmonica Aces:
Tommy Leddy, Oliver Sinnott, Donal Stewart, Ownie Raferty, Ken Donnelly,
Teddy McConnon.

CHAPTER THIRTEEN

"NO JITTERBUGGING"

Our next gig was in St Bridget's Hall in Drogheda, which was also the venue for "Parish Nights". As well as variety shows and dances, St. Bridgets also catered for the younger generation by holding a weekly "Hop". I suppose the present day equivalent of a "Hop" would be a disco.

As we approached the front door we were greeted by a very large poster which read "Strictly no Jitterbugging" (otherwise known as jiving etc.). I remember thinking that the likelihood of anyone being ejected for breaking this rule during our performance was rather remote.

I can't remember much about the gig itself but I most definitely remember the comments of a certain female neighbour of mine, a girl called Imelda. When I innocently asked her what she thought of our performance the previous night, she rather discouragingly replied, "The band was poxy".

Undeterred, we carried on playing under the same name, and using the same band format.

Several other outfits were not as concerned about such formalities. They regularly changed both the personnel and the band name.

I know of one band who played at a gig in County Kerry and were so bad that the furious organisers threatened to call the cops if they ever showed their faces there again.

On the journey home from the gig, they decided on a further name change and then placed an advertisement in the national newspapers seeking new bookings. Guess who that same Kerry committee booked for their following Sunday night dance?

Needless to say, our heroes duly showed up. The hapless dance committee were left with no alternative but to let them take to the stage. At the end of the night, and presumably because nobody would have anything to do with the band, the fee for the gig was thrown on a table by the exit door.

When confirming dance bookings, it was fairly common practice for some committees to ask band managers to supply details of how many members they had in their band's line-up. Presumably this information was required for advertisement purposes, and did not usually present any problem.

However, for one particular band manager, who shall remain nameless, this question regularly presented him with a major headache. For example, he might have claimed in his application letter that he had a seven piece outfit only to discover on the day of the gig that he was somewhat short of this number.

The sight of his band wagon in the car park of the local church was a regular feature on most Sunday mornings. Many a musician heard that fateful call "are you ok for Kerry tonight", or indeed any other far flung county in the country, as he desperately attempted to press-gang someone for his band.

On one such Sunday morning, when he had successfully recruited six musicians, but still required a double bass player to complete the line-up, he approached a well known drummer and singer and asked him if he could play this instrument. While not generally known as a bass player, he said that he knew where he could get his hands on one and he agreed to give it a go.

The gig went ok, but the most memorable part of the evening was the sight of our hastily recruited double bass player deftly running his fingers up and down the strings of the instrument, while crooning "Boom, Boom, Boom, Boom, Boom, Boom, Boom, Boom," into the microphone. He spent much of the evening elegantly spinning the instrument around in his hands, for which he received great applause from the audience. He quite simply mesmerised them with his skills, and was the star of the show. It was only after the gig had ended, we discovered that the double bass had no strings attached to it, and instead, it simply had four straight lines drawn along its neck.

CHAPTER FOURTEEN

GETTING BETTER

following a few personnel changes, and more importantly, a name change (we changed our name to the Checkmates), we began to make significant improvement. We even had new band uniforms which were made for us by saxophone player Patsy Dowd's mother Roseanne. Nevertheless, it was still an uphill struggle to survive. With little or no bookings to fulfil, we decided to concentrate on a period of intensive band practice. The Whitworth Hall, although still open, was no longer used as a dance venue, and we hired one of the vacant rooms there for our band rehearsals.

In those days the preparation for a band rehearsal was rather simple. The most popular radio station of the day was Radio Luxembourg, and one or more of the band members would be given the job of recording some of its shows. The tape recordings of various songs were played on rehearsal night,

The Checkmates:
Sean Donnelly, Ben Moonan, Jim Carton, Frankie Smith
Patsy Dowd, Harry O'Reilly (author) Paddy Byrne.

and the most suitable of them were then selected. The rest of the night was spent listening to, and then learning to play the songs, for their inclusion in our dance programme.

One of the first gigs Ben Moonan managed to secure for us was a 9pm to 2am dance in Listowel in Co. Kerry. The venue was "The White Horse Inn", and was owned by the colourful international singing star Joseph Locke.

We confidently set out on the 500 mile round trip to Listowel, armed with our new line-up, new repertoire, and new uniforms. The band was quite well received but otherwise the gig was unremarkable.

What was remarkable about this night was that we received our fee by cheque, and on our homeward journey, when we stopped at an all night cafe, we had to pool what little cash we had in order to buy a couple of bags of chips. Later on that day when Ben presented the cheque for payment at his bank, as you've probably already guessed by now, the cheque bounced.

Ben was an extremely nice guy, and he paid us by cash from his own pocket, but sadly I suspect that the cheque was never honoured.

During the early 1960s the formats of the bands were constantly changing. There were numerous musicians coming and going. Many of them were generally known as journey men.

Not long after the Listowel escapade, when our regular sax player suffered a bout of 'flu, we enlisted the talents of one such musician. He was an extremely good sax player, but unfortunately he had fallen on hard times. On hiring him for the gig, it was necessary to retrieve his saxophone from the local pawn shop.

On arrival at the venue, as was usual, the big boys went to the pub for a drink, while Frankie Smith and I stayed behind to set up our equipment for the evening. Our intrepid saxophonist was wearing a distinctly unkempt shirt, which we both commented upon. Suddenly, to our amazement, he opened his saxophone case, produced an immaculate false front for his shirt complete with bow tie, tucked it inside his trousers and was immediately transformed from looking like a roadie to being mistaken for our band leader.

It was during my time with The Checkmates that I learned to play guitar and I gradually introduced guitar playing alongside my accordion playing. Two of the new band recruits were Frankie Smith (trumpet) and Jim Carton (singer). I continued my association with Frankie as we pursued our musical careers with local bands but Jim Carton decided that his future career lay elsewhere.

I first met Jim when we were rivals in the final of yet another talent contest, where I played solo accordion, and he was accompanied by three musicians,

The Jim Carton Group:
Patsy Carton, Jim Carton, Paddy Farrell, Gerry Saurin

who were also good friends of mine, Patsy Carton and Gerry Saurin (both from Tullyallen), and Paddy Farrell from Laytown. This was a major competition and the contestants came from all over Ireland. The compere for the final show was the well known actor and singer Joe Lynch. It was held in Dublin's old Theatre Royal. The first prize included a guarantee of an appearance on the newly opened Telefis Eireann.

The winners were the comedy duo Tom and Pascal, who went on to host their own TV series. The runner-up was Dickie Rock who of course became a household name due to his fantastic success with the Miami Showband and also as a solo artist. Unfortunately, Jim and I were among the remaining ten unsuccessful finalists.

Prior to his showband career, Jim had been a lead soloist with St. Peter's Church Choir, under the guidance of its renowned director and organist Eugene Mooney.

His career really took off following his departure to Canada in 1967. As lead vocalist with "The Jimmy Carton Band", he performed extensively across Canada and the U.S., where he now has a huge fan base. His stage shows invariably attract sell out audiences and he is also a major recording artist with several successful albums to his name.

Regardless of all his commercial success, Jim still returns regularly to perform with choirs or as a soloist in churches and cathedrals throughout North America.

CHAPTER FIFTEEN

GOODBYE ACCORDION, HELLO GUITAR

Before I learned to play guitar, but while still occasionally playing accordion with dance bands, I continued my education as a pupil at the local Christian Brothers School in Drogheda. It was around this time that we formed the C.B.S. accordion band. This band may have only lasted for a very short time, but a few of the members went on to become well known figures on the entertainment scene, not only as accordionists, but particularly as guitarists, and it is with this in mind that I will single out a few for special mention.

Three of the musicians, Paddy Farrell (Laytown), Patsy Carton (Tullyallen) and of course myself, were members of the school band, but Eamonn Campbell, although not a member of this band, was a school pal of mine at the time and would soon feature very prominently with us during our guitar playing days. At one time or another, but not at the same time, we each played guitar with Louis Smith and his "Delta Boys" Showband.

I think it's fair to say that Paddy Farrell was the first one of us to be acclaimed for his guitar playing ability, and I would like to add that he was very helpful in passing on quite a lot of his knowledge, not only to us, but to many other budding guitarists of that time. Well known guitarist Phil (Birch) McLoughlin from Bettystown, would no doubt endorse this view.

Paddy played with several outfits during the 1960s including Dermot O'Brien and The Clubmen, before taking his talents to America, where he achieved tremendous success. When I told "Birch" McLoughlin that I was featuring Paddy in this book, he in turn told Paddy's family in Bettystown,

Paddy Farrell (Laytown)

and they very kindly let me have a photograph together with a tribute to him which appeared in The New York Irish Echo newspaper.

I have detailed my own personal knowledge of Paddy, but in order to demonstrate the high regard in which he was held during his American career, I have reproduced some extracts from this excellent newspaper article.

"There's a quaint little village on the East Meath shore its beautiful strand stretches ten miles or more". These are the opening lines of Paddy Farrell's own composition of "Sweet Bettystown", which of course is a beautiful song about his home town in Co. Meath. No matter where his musical travels took him he still considered that quaint little village his very own home which has sadly now become his final earthly resting place.

The writer of the article says that he had known about Paddy through his membership of Dermot O'Brien's Clubmen in Ireland and also through his membership of The Jesse Owens Band in New York. However, his first encounter with Paddy was at a New York venue called "The John Barleycorn", where Paddy was performing with Charlie Magee. It was during a conversation following the gig that Charlie introduced them, and referred to Paddy as the "king of the diminished chord". This encounter led to a long lasting friendship. Paddy also had many recording credits to his name with Dermot O'Brien, Jesse Owens, and Noel Kingston.

The article is quite extensive about Paddy's time in America, but I am sure that the writer would like me to reproduce his concluding tribute to Paddy; "The night sky is not as brilliant as before, because one of the greatest stars of the Irish American scene shines no more".

Musicians Night Out: Boyne Rovers Club: Derek McCormack, Jim Kavanagh, Kenny Doyle, Val Rogers, Harry Martin, Paul Martin, Brendan Crean, Brendan Goring, Roy McCormack, John (Twick) Donnelly, Brendan Hoey, Terry Smith.

The New Sound:
Roy McCormack, Jim Kavanagh, John (Twick) Donnelly, Kenny Doyle.

CHAPTER SIXTEEN

EAMONN MAKES HIS MARK

When Eamonn Campbell decided to take up guitar playing, both Paddy Farrell and Patsy Carton were already quite proficient guitarists. Shortly after he acquired his first guitar, Eamonn met up with the Farrell brothers, Larry and Paddy (another Paddy Farrell), from The Greenlanes in Drogheda, both of whom had recently begun playing guitar, and they invited him to their home. The Farrell brothers had an extensive record collection and this proved invaluable to an aspiring guitarist. However, they played their guitars with an open style tuning which was sometimes referred to as Hawaiian guitar tuning. Eamonn soon realised that he would have to learn to play guitar with the more widely used Spanish guitar tuning. To this end, he received guitar lessons from Frank Cassidy at Patrick Street Drogheda, where he also learned to read music. To further his music studies, he attended the Brass and Reed Band's junior music school, where he received tuition from musicians Syd Kierans and Christy Smith.

It was around this time, 1960/61, that he invited me to bring my accordion along to his house and to join him in a guitar/

Eamonn Campbell:

Eamonn Campbell and the Dubliners:
Eamonn on Stage with the Dubliners. (photograph courtesy of Peter Schittler.)

accordion duet. It was also during these visits that I began to take a shine to the guitar, and as it was the glamour musical instrument of the day, I soon decided to give it a go.

In the early days we shared Eamonn's guitar and we also shared a guitar tuition book. We generally practised together in the living room of Eamonn's house where he had a very modern hi-fi system. He also had several recordings of The Shadows guitar tunes, which we played tirelessly as we tried to emulate them.

As I was playing my accordion with The Checkmates Showband at this time, I encouraged Eamonn to accompany us on some of our gigs, while he also kept himself busy by playing with another local Showband called Jimmy Waters and The Viceroys.

Following Eamonn's recruitment to Louis Smith's Delta Boys Showband, I began to introduce my own guitar playing into The Checkmates dance programme.

Despite my parent's misgivings about me taking up guitar playing and possibly reducing my future accordion prospects, I managed to persuade them to let me have my own guitar.

As I was a teenager at that time, and as most teenagers wanted to be guitar players, the inevitable happened and I found myself concentrating almost entirely on my guitar playing.

I still remember my accordion teacher Cyril Jolley telling me that in his opinion the popularity of guitar playing would soon fizzle out, because, unlike accordion playing, it was just a passing fad. Undeterred I carried on, and just like Eamonn, I am still playing guitar today.

Although our careers took different paths, I remained as a part-time musician and followed a full-time career with The Post Office, while Eamonn pursued his career as a full-time musician, we have always remained good friends and I am very happy to give a short account of his subsequent glittering career.

Eamonn continued to play with Louis Smiths' Delta Boys until early 1964 and on his departure from this outfit he joined the Bee Vee Five.

Incidentally, Louis Smith invited me to fill the guitarist vacancy created by Eamonn's departure, and during my time with that band, together with Louis' guidance, my guitar playing improved significantly.

When Eamonn exited the Bee Vee Five in November 1964 to join Dermot O'Brien's Clubmen, it was also the beginning of his new career as a full time professional musician.

In May 1968, when The Clubmen and Dermot O'Brien decided to end their association, Dermot continued with his solo career, while The Clubmen changed the name of their outfit to "The Tigermen Showband". (I will include a separate report on this outfit elsewhere). Eamonn continued to play with The Tigermen until 1970 when, following a two year separation, Dermot and The Clubmen decided to get together again and resume their previously successful partnership.

It was also during 1970 that Eamonn joined Harry Martin and The Country Gents, and although I have already reviewed this group, I should also mention that Eamonn played with both groups during this period, and the bookings were organised to facilitate this arrangement.

In 1973 Eamonn left Dermot and began work in both Eamonn Andrews and Trend Studios as a session musician. He later joined the RTE Orchestra where he did lots of Television work. He played at The Gaiety Theatre for their Gaels of Laughter series with Maureen Potter. He also played with the concert orchestras for "Joseph And His Amazing Technicolour Dreamcoat", "Jesus Christ Superstar", and "West Side Story".

He regularly accompanied Tony Kenny and Brendan Grace, and he was Musical Director and Producer for Brendan Shine's Nice and Easy TV series. He is also regarded as one of Ireland's most successful record producers. He produced hits for Paddy Reilly, Foster and Allen, Brendan Grace, Daniel O'Donnell, Brendan Shine, Philomena Begley, and more recently, American country singer Billy Jo Spears.

During a U.K. tour in 1967, Dermot O'Brien and The Clubmen shared the bill with The Dubliners, and it was during some of the after-show sessions that Eamonn developed a long lasting friendship with The Dubliners. He made numerous guest appearances with the group, joining them on a full-time basis in 1987 when they performed their 25th anniversary show on "The Late Late Show" hosted by Gay Byrne.

He produced The Dubliners 25 Years double album, and he was instrumental in bringing together The Pogues and The Dubliners for their recording of The Irish Rover, which they performed on Top Of The Pops In 1987.

In 1991 he produced the recording of Rory Gallagher and The Dubliners entitled "Barley and The Grape Rag", and this was most likely Rory's last commercial recording.

Finally, when I asked Eamonn to select a personal favourite memory from his wonderful career, without hesitation he told me that he had two particular favourites. He described playing with Rory Gallagher as being absolutely amazing, and he put this on a par with the great honour he felt at being selected as Grand Master for the St. Patrick's Day Parade in his home town of Drogheda in 2009.

The Toppers:
Podger Reynolds, Ken Donnelly, Tommy Moonan, Johnny Milne, Tommy Leddy (Bass) Mall Caffrey, Pascal Mooney.

CHAPTER SEVENTEEN

PODGER AND THE TOPPERS

My own career with The Checkmates came to an end in 1963, when I successfully auditioned for the position of lead guitarist with The Toppers Showband.

This band had evolved from the original outfit which took part in the previously mentioned "Parish Nights" competition. The name of the band was adopted from the title of a well-known children's comic book of that time, "The Topper".

The band had undergone several personnel changes during the intervening period, and the original four piece line-up had been increased to that of a

The Toppers Showband:
Tommy Leddy, Pascal Mooney, Ken Donnelly, Podger Reynolds,
Johnny Milne, Mal Caffrey, Tommy Moonan.

Paddy (Podger) Reynolds & The Casino Showband with the Rolling Stones.

seven piece outfit. They had also become very successful and had a significant fan base, but before I give an account of my time with this band, I must refer to some relevant background information on some of The Toppers' former members.

Paddy (Podger) Reynolds was the first of the founder members to leave the band. In 1960 he joined the Abbey Ballroom Orchestra, and following his departure from this band, he took the decision to become a full time professional musician.

Paddy (Podger) Reynolds

He began his professional career with The Maurice Lynch Showband. This was to be just the beginning of a wonderful career in entertainment, and his tenor saxophone playing coupled with his excellent vocals soon earned him the title of "The Great Showman". He gained quite a reputation with The Maurice Lynch Band and in 1963 he took up an offer to join the Dublin based Casino Showband. I heard this band on some of their many visits to Drogheda's Abbey Ballroom, and they were indeed top class.

One of their more memorable gigs came about when they were hired to play support band for The Rolling Stones in Belfast in the mid-1960s. I have included a photograph which was taken at the event.

In 1968 Podger joined another leading outfit called the Pacific Showband, and one year later his career took another major turn when this band decided on a permanent move to Canada. They were based in Toronto and the band changed its name to The Dublin Corporation. They enjoyed great success and

Paddy (Podger) Reynolds

built up a huge Canadian fan base. They continued with their recording career, and as well as having three hit single records, they recorded an album which secured a place in the Canadian top ten album charts.

Yet more success awaited Podger when in 1975, he joined The Big 8 Showband in Las Vegas, where they were billed as The Irish Showband.

Having reached the dizzy heights of show business, he remained with this band until 1985, before deciding on a much quieter lifestyle, and a return home to Ireland.

Malachy (Mal) Caffrey was the second of the original members to leave

The Toppers, and I was recruited to fill this vacancy. Mal decided to leave the band in order to devote all of his time to the promotion of his own fledgling business known as Caffreys Monumental Works and to turn it into the thriving enterprise that it is today. Both Tommy Leddy and Tommy Moonan remained with the band throughout its existence.

Willie Walsh also followed Podger's lead and embarked on a career as a full time professional musician. The vacancy created by his departure from The Toppers was filled by my old pal from The Checkmates, Frankie Smith. Willie teamed up with such showbands as Des Smith and The Collegemen, and following his departure from this band, he was invited to join The Nevada Showband. The Nevada was without doubt one of Ireland's leading outfits during the 1960s and featured several leading vocalists of the era, including Kelly, Roly Daniels, and Red Hurley. Willie went on to enjoy a long and successful career in show business until his well earned retirement some years ago.

I am pleased to say that I have shared a stage with Podger, Mal, and Willie at various times, usually whenever they were available to make guest appearances with The Toppers.

Musicians night out in Sharkeys, Clogherhead:
Shaun Reynolds, Tony Barrett, Paddy Farrell (Laytown) Gerry Hughes,
Brendan Crean.

Fintan Stanley, Louis Smith, Brendan Crean,
at the Black Bull Inn, Drogheda.

CHAPTER EIGHTEEN

BARRY CLUSKEY
JAZZ SUPREMO

This seems like an appropriate place to include a brief summary of the wonderful career of Barry Cluskey (saxophonist/clarinetist), another outstanding Drogheda musician with a similar profile to that of Podger Reynolds but who, unfortunately, I did not have the opportunity to share a stage with. Nevertheless, I have known Barry for many years, and have witnessed many of his superb performances.

Like so many other local musicians, Barry enrolled with The Drogheda Brass & Reed Band, where he began his musical career by taking Trumpet-

Barry Cluskey

The Cluskey Hopkins Jazz Band

The Kings Showband with Barry Cluskey

playing lessons. However, from the outset, Barry really wanted to learn to play the saxophone, and as his brother was already an accomplished saxophonist, with a collection of records which included many featuring Jazz legend Benny Goodman, he soon dropped the idea of trumpet playing and began learning to play the saxophone instead. He learned very well, because today he is ranked amongst the top exponents of both the saxophone and clarinet, not just in Ireland, but also on the international stage.

He played saxophone with a few local bands such as The Flying Aces and the Silver Seven before graduating to his first jazz band. This outfit became known as The Jazz Notes, and was a four piece outfit comprised of Barry (saxophone), Ralph Lynch (vocals & double bass), Johnny Barton (drums), and Dessie McManus (keyboards). The band enjoyed quite a successful career, during which they played at many venues around the local circuit. They were also featured regularly on stage at The Abbey Ballroom.

At the beginning of the 1960s, Barry decided to pursue a career as a full time professional musician, and to this end he successfully auditioned for the position of saxophonist with Paddy Kearns and The Boyne Valley Stompers. This outfit provided him with a great start to his new professional career, and the experience which he gained would prove to be invaluable in his future spectacular career, both as a band leader and an internationally renowned jazz musician. He remained with The Paddy Kearns Jazz outfit for about one year, and in early 1961 he embarked on a significant career change when he became the leader and founding member of The Kings Showband. Incidentally, his replacement with The Boyne Valley Stompers was none other than his good friend Podger Reynolds.

The Kings Showband established their base in Naas, Co. Kildare, and they were very soon ranked amongst the top ten outfits in the country. They built up a huge fan base, and they remained in demand throughout Ireland during the 1960s. After a few years, the band decided to broaden their horizon by embarking on a number of foreign tours. They toured extensively throughout England and America, regularly supporting many international stars such as

Little Richard and Bill Haley, but it was at home in Ireland, at a gig in Banbridge Co. Down, that legendary American Rock Star Jerry Lee Lewis invited Barry to join his band on stage. Jerry Lee was so impressed by Barry's performance that he offered him a full time position with his band. Unfortunately, as the job would require Barry to re-locate to America on a permanent basis, he reluctantly decided to decline this most enticing offer.

In 1967, The King's succeeded in recruiting Butch Moore to their line-up. Butch was by then one of Ireland's leading singing stars, and had already notched up a string of record successes to his name. He had, of course, earlier represented Ireland in the 1965 Eurovision Song Contest in Naples.

The Kings Showband remained at the top of the ratings until their eventual disbandment at the beginning of the 1970s. They made several successful recordings during the 1960s, most notable being their 1966 version of the Stephen Foster song Beautiful Dreamer, which, following significant British airplay on radio Caroline, was a major chart success. However, the end of The Kings Showband led to the beginning of a fantastically successful career-change for Barry, when he decided to return to his beloved jazz scene.

Prior to the demise of The Kings Showband, Barry and fellow band members Des Hopkins (drums), and Billy Hopkins (bass) were already the core members of a jazz outfit which they had managed to run in tandem with their membership of The Kings. Following the dissolution of the showband they decided to embark on a full time career as a jazz band, and to this end, they adopted the name of The Cluskey Hopkins Jazz Band. The line-up consisted of Barry (saxophone/clarinet), Des (drums), Billy Hopkins (bass), Dougie O'Brien (trombone), Paul Harte (piano), and Mike (Magic) Henry (trumpet).

They soon became established amongst the elite of the jazz fraternity, and their stage performances, at both national and international venues, received widespread acclaim. Their outstanding stage shows at The Guinness sponsored Cork Jazz Festivals during the late 1970s and early 1980s attracted the attention of the sponsors, and they were invited to represent The Guinness Company at Jazz Festivals throughout the world. They accepted the company's very

The Barry Cluskey Group:
John (Twick) Donnelly, Barry Cluskey, Pa Carter, Raphael Carr – (1960)

attractive offer, and the group subsequently became known as The Cluskey Hopkins Guinness Jazz Show.

This arrangement continues up to the present day, and over the ensuing years, Barry and Co. have been joined on stage by many international stars including Johnny Dankworth, Aker Bilk, Kenny Ball, George Melly, and Louis Stewart. The group have made numerous recordings over the years, and not least amongst them is Barry's version of The Aker Bilk smash hit Stranger On The Shore. One night when the group were performing with the great man himself, Barry asked Aker if he would like to join him on stage for a rendition of this tune. Aker agreed but graciously insisted that Barry should take the lead role in its performance. However, Barry's clarinet solo must have been rather good, because, half way through his performance, Aker muttered in jest, "stop showing off you ****"!

The Cluskey Hopkins Guinness Jazz Show continues to grace concert stages throughout the world, and will hopefully continue to do so for many more years.

The Toppers Showband:
Back – Paddy Toner, Johnny Milne, Tommy Leddy, Jim Delaney, Gene Clinton,
Willie Walsh, Mickey Rooney.

Toppers Reunion:
Tommy Leddy, Johnny Milne, Podger Reynolds, Ken Donnelly, Tommy Moonan,
Frankie Smith, Willie Walsh, Mal Caffrey.

CHAPTER NINETEEN

BALLROOM OF ROMANCE AND THE ROMANTIC INTERLUDE

following a successful audition, I was offered the position of lead guitarist with The Nevada Showband. As this band were full-time professionals, it was necessary for me to give up my full time day job with the Post Office, and embark on a new career as a full time professional musician. This proved to be a very difficult decision to make, but when the crunch time came, I got cold feet and reluctantly declined the offer from the band.

On joining The Toppers Showband, I had my first encounter with the two guys who were the inspiration for this book - Paddy Toner (drums), and Mickey Rooney (vocalist).

The musicians who made up the seven piece band were Tommy Leddy (bass guitar), Johnny Milne (trombone), Tommy Moonan (saxophone), Frankie Smith (trumpet) and me. I should add here that it took a bit of persuasion to encourage Frankie to transfer from The Checkmates to The Toppers, but just like me he felt that it was a good time to move on.

The band had a fairly extensive repertoire, together with quite a number of confirmed bookings in the diary, and we were able to use this as a launch pad for the new line-up. Our immediate priority was to begin an intense series of rehearsals to enable us to satisfactorily fulfil the existing commitments, and hopefully expand our diary of engagements.

The format for The Toppers rehearsals was very similar to that of The Checkmates and was most likely the same for almost all bands of the emerging showband era. The days when music scores had to be obtained, or written, were sadly becoming a rarity, and were generally only used by the few remaining

The Toppers Showband: Tommy Moonan, Tommy Leddy, Johnny Milne, Mickey Rooney, Frankie Smith, Harry O'Reilly, Paddy Toner. (In The Abbey Ballroom, Drogheda)

orchestras still in existence.

As the band was well established, there were quite a few regular, or what we called return gigs in the diary, and one of my first appearances with them was a dance venue in Glenfarne in Co. Leitrim.

The dance hall was known as the Ballroom of Romance, the same dance hall that featured in the film of the same name. However, as the film was made decades later, I will relate the story as seen by me at first hand.

It was a Sunday night gig, and as we travelled in our band wagon on the two hundred mile round trip to Glenfarne, apart from the usual banter, there were two topics which dominated the back seat discussions.

The first one concerned the bands previous journey here, which occurred during a snow storm. The area is surrounded by some very hilly terrain, with steep drops on either side of the road. There are little or no hedges or roadside safety barriers to provide protection, and should any unfortunate vehicle leave the road, then a very sticky end is in store. This was pointed out to me as we travelled through the area, and I definitely agreed with them.

They recalled how they shouted obscenities at our regular van driver Tommy Leddy, as he ignored all calls to halt the wagon while they continually skidded perilously close to the edges of both sides of the road. They believed that Tommy was enjoying their discomfort, as some of them recited rosaries, while others threatened to jump out of the wagon.

The memory of that particular night stirred a fresh barrage of abuse and threats of all kinds aimed at Tommy, should he ever again attempt to pull a similar stunt.

When tempers cooled down, we moved on to the second topic which concerned the upcoming gig. I asked the usual questions such as, what sort of an audience might we expect, and how many of them might show up etc. I was told that Glenfarne was very typical of most country dance halls of that time, and although the area appeared to be very sparsely populated, we were assured of a big crowd due to the band's popularity and also the drawing power of the venue itself.

Dec 30th	Omagh	£20-0-0		Jan 62	
	Band	10-10-0	Jan 1st	Gorey	£35-0-0
	Taxi & Amps	9-0-0		Band	£21-0-0
	Manager & Promoter	2-0-0		Taxi & Amps	£10-0-0
	Balance	1-10-0		Manager	£1-15-0
	Money Owed	7-16-9		Caretaker	£5-0
	Balance Owed	9-6-9		Balance	£2-0-0
Dec 31st	Cahir	£40-0-0		Money Owed	6-6-9
	Manager	2-0-0		Balance Owed	£4-6-9
	Committee	1-0-0	Jan 7th	Ballyleagh	£30-0-0
	Band	21-0-0		Band	17-10-0
	Taxis & Amps	13-0-0		Taxi & Amps	9-0-0
	Balance	£3-0-0		Manager	1-10-0
	Money Owed	9-6-9		Balance	£2-0-0
	Balance Owed	6-6-9		Money Owed	£4-6-9
				Balance Owed	£2-6-9
			Jan 9th	Navan	£12-10-0
				Band	£10-10-0
				Taxi & Amps	3-0-0
				Balance	£1-0-0
				Money Owed	£2-6-9
				Balance Owed	£3-6-9

Diary Extracts 1962

Sun Oct 29th	Longford	£30-0-0	Nov 5th	Carlow	£30-0-0
	Band	14-10-0		Band	17-10-0
	Taxi & Amps	9-0-0		Taxi & Amps	9-0-0
	Manager	1-10-0		Manager	1-10-0
		£2-0-0		Balance	£2-0-0
	Taken Over	£8-2-3		Taken Over	10-12-3
	Balance	£10-2-3		Balance	12-12-3
	Caretaker	£1-0-0		Drogheda Panto	10-0
	Balance	£9-2-3		Balance	12-2-3
Tues Oct 31	Malahide	£25-0-0		[illegible]	16-6
	Band	£14-0-0		Balance	£11-5-9
	Taxi & Amp	£4-0-0	Nov 12th	Glenfarne	£35-0-0
	Manager	£1-5-0		Band	[illegible]
	Money toward debt	£5-0-0		Manager & Suppers	4-0-0
	Balance	£0-15-0		Taxi & Amps	11-0-0
	Taken over	£9-2-3		Balance	1-0-0
	Balance	£9-17-3		Taken over	11-5-9
Wed Nov 1st	Navan	£15-0-0		Balance	10-5-9
	Money toward Debt	10-0-0		Band Practice	16-6
	Taxi & Amps J. Donnelly	3-10-0		Balance	£9-9-3
	Manager	15-0		Timber for Stand	1-3-9
	Balance	5-0		Balance	8-5-6
	Taken over	9-14-3			
	Balance	10-12-3			

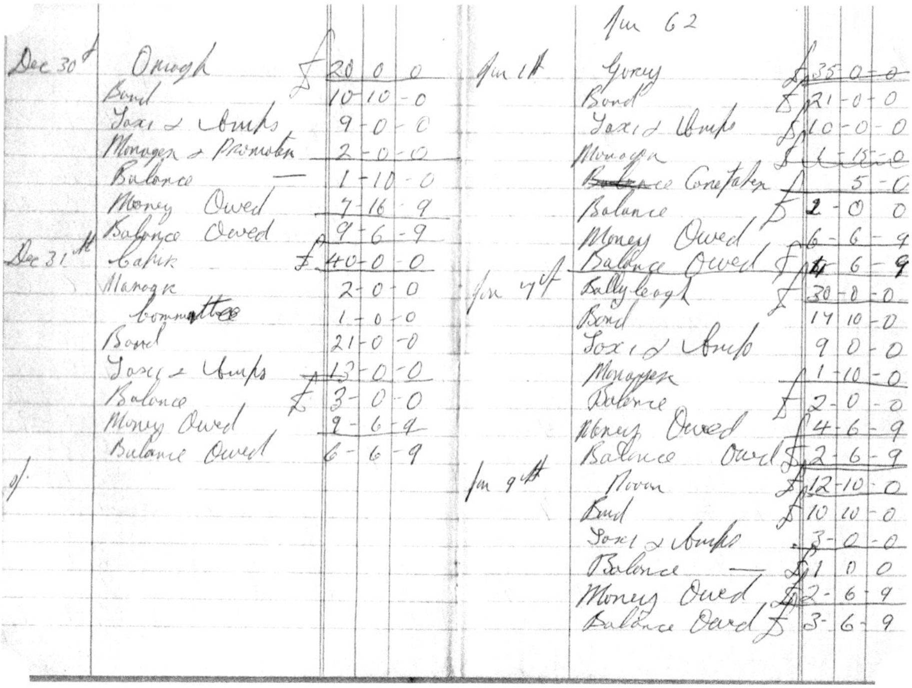

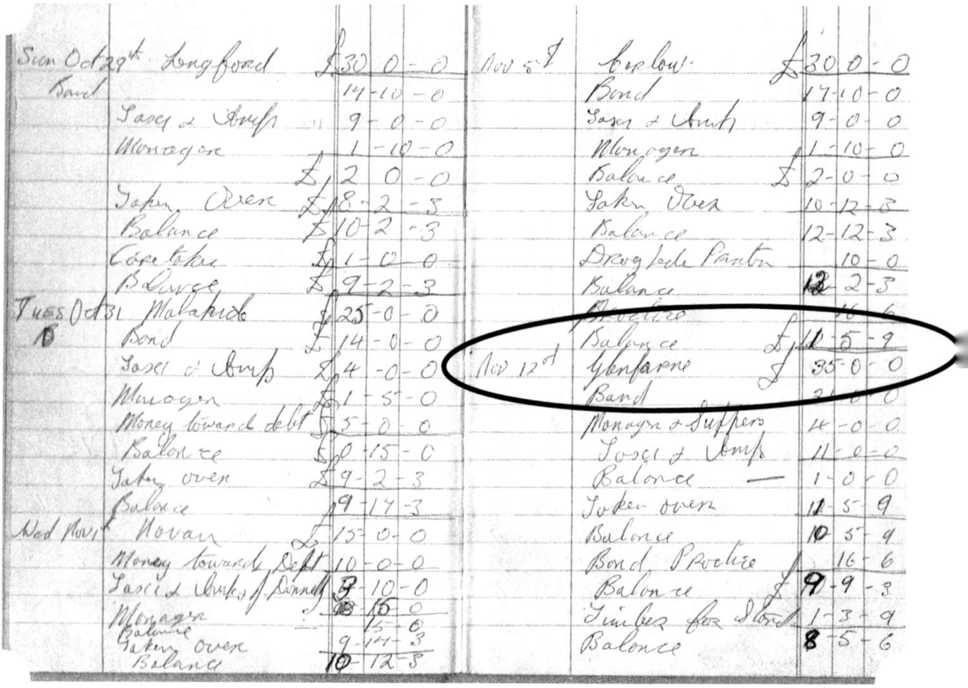

Diary Extracts

I was told that the popularity of the venue was due in no small part to a certain gentleman who was known simply as John, who would join us on stage sometime during the night.

The night began with a steady flow of people filtering in to the hall, and as the numbers increased quite considerably, they began to assemble on either side of the hall, ladies on one side and gents on the other. This situation would not be considered very unusual at many other rural dance venues, but despite our best efforts on the stage, the assembled audience seemed content to stand in orderly lines on either side of the dance floor.

Suddenly a guy in a tuxedo stepped forward through the crowd and on to the stage. "Right lads time for our romantic interlude". He asked us to play a selection of slow dances, while he took control of one of our microphones, and throughout our performances he spoke directly to the assembled audience. He addressed them individually with words of encouragement from the stage like "Jimmy ye're looking very smart tonight, I think Mary over there would agree with me", followed by, "What do ye think Mary, would ye not agree with me, don't let me down now when he asks ye to dance". Then he returns to the hapless Jimmy and tells him, "I think you'll be ok now Jimmy boy". Amazingly, Jimmy crosses the floor and takes Mary out to dance.

John continued with the same routine of singling out ladies and gents and addressing them personally. He kept moving along both sets of ladies and gents until the dance floor was crammed with dancers, and then he vanished as quickly as he had appeared.

The band played several more gigs there, and on each occasion, John never failed to put in an appearance.

Glenfarne marked the start of a weekly ritual of long distance trips to dances which took me to the four corners of Ireland, and just like Glenfarne, they nearly always took place on a Sunday night. Not only was Sunday the most practical day for undertaking long distance journeys, but it was also by far the most popular night for dancing, anywhere in Ireland. We tried to keep our weekday gigs within a 50 mile radius of home.

The Toppers Showband:
Willie Walsh, Tommy Leddy, Gene Clinton, Tommy Moonan, Ken Donnelly,
Johnny Milne, Mal Caffrey.

The Toppers Showband:
Tommy Leddy, Mal Caffrey, Willie Walsh, Tommy Moonan,
Johnny Milne, Gene Clinton, Ken Donnelly.

CHAPTER TWENTY

ON THE ROAD WITH THE TOPPERS

Tommy Leddy, our bass player and driver, usually undertook the task of safely getting us to and from the gigs, and as our regular manager Oliver Mullen rarely travelled with us, Tommy assumed the "on the road" managerial responsibilities for the band.

Oliver had previously acted as a dance promoter for the Whitworth Hall, before assuming the role of manager for The Toppers, and although he disliked travelling with the band, he insisted on seeing us off on our Sunday afternoon travels. He liked to exercise his authority by issuing various instructions to Tommy regarding the gig in question, before turning to the rest of us and irritatingly rubbing his hands while gleefully shouting "ok boys, bring home the lolly". Predictably, he always got a mention or two during the subsequent band wagon conversations.

However, on the few occasions when Tommy was unable to travel, due to illness or holidays, Oliver took over as our driver, and on each of these occasions we ended up with one crisis or another. Thankfully, as Tommy was a very healthy individual and only took holidays once a year these occasions were very rare and probably amounted to no more than three or four times overall.

Tommy was a teetotaller, while most of the other lads enjoyed a drink or three, so as long as he was present, a degree of order and decorum was maintained during the course of each night. On the other hand, Oliver enjoyed a drink and often socialised with some of the lads, and this was not at all a very good arrangement.

In order to demonstrate this, I will relate the events of two such gigs. The first of these evenings, which remain etched in my memory, occurred when we were en route to a gig in the village of Monaseed in Co.Wicklow in 1964. With just 10 more miles of our journey remaining, Oliver pointed to a roadside pub and asked if anyone would like to stop for a quick drink. He received a unanimous roar of approval as we called in to the pub and the lads proceeded to order copious amounts of beer. They even performed several songs for the entertainment of the locals.

As Frankie and I were the only non drinkers present, we became worried about the behaviour of the rest of the band. We really began to panic when we realised that the time was 9.30pm and the dance had been scheduled to commence half an hour earlier at 9.00pm. We bundled them into the van and hurriedly travelled the remaining 10 miles to the gig.

We were hoping that this was one of those dance halls where the patrons were not too punctual, and hopefully would not arrive until long after the advertised time of the dance. No such luck. The hall was already packed with hundreds of punters. We made some feeble excuse about incurring a couple of punctures, as we rushed backstage and hurriedly struggled to put on our band uniforms. The stage area of the hall was surrounded with some old style scenery props. These were still in place following the performance of a parochial variety concert held there during the previous week. As one of the lads was pulling up the trousers of his uniform, he lost his balance and fell against a section of the scenery causing it to collapse outwards on to the stage. He then fell out onto the stage minus his trousers. The fallen scenery piece also left a gaping hole through which the rest of us were left exposed in various stages of undress. The audience looked on in astonishment as we hastily tried to compose ourselves. We did our best to put the incident behind us, and we performed as professionally as possible under the circumstances. We also agreed to play a full four hour programme to compensate for our late start.
That was surely the longest four hours we have ever had to endure. I don't know what the organisers said to Oliver, but we definitely did not receive a

return invitation.

The second occasion when Tommy was unable to travel with us occurred on the Whit Bank Holiday weekend of that same year. We were booked to play on the Sunday night in Ennis in Co. Clare, and as we had no work to go to on the holiday Monday, we decided to postpone our return journey. We made arrangements to stay overnight in the town, and this situation appealed to us because it gave us the feeling of being fulltime professional musicians.

As I recall, there was a big crowd in attendance, and the band was really well received. There was a sense of relief following the gig, relieved of the drudgery of loading the band wagon and having to rush headlong across the country in an effort to be in time for our day jobs the following morning.

In those days it was quite a regular occurrence to bypass the homes of some of the lads and to drive them directly to work. The lack of a proper night's sleep, not to mention having to go to work with a breakfast consisting of a few sandwiches they had prepared the night before and taken with them in the band wagon, made the Monday morning blues even more dreadful for these part-time bandsmen.

No such feelings on this night. We were all very upbeat following our successful performance, and the dance committee treated us to a rather large supply of refreshments. We spent a few hours socialising before retiring to our accommodation, which was only one mile from the dance hall.

Following a good night's sleep, we arose bright and early next morning - well at least some of us did. Some of the lads were suffering the after affects of the previous night's performance, not to mention the consumption of the generous supply of late night refreshments. Some of us enjoyed a hearty breakfast, while the others checked out the nearest early-opening boozer.

So began an all morning session of drink, cigarettes, and betting on horses, and of course the lads provided an impromptu concert for the locals in the pub. Oliver eventually decided that we should head for home, and we all piled into the van and raced down the Dublin road.

Before long we had to stop to spend a penny. Oliver parked the van on the

PLAY IT AGAIN PADDY

hard shoulder of the main Limerick to Dublin road. Everyone agreed that one of the lads in particular was very much "the worse for wear", and in order to spare his blushes, I have decided not to mention his name. However, following their visit to a secluded spot in a field by the roadside, a terrible vision emerged at the gate of the field. It was Oliver carrying this guy in his arms. The guy's trousers were down round his ankles, and the belt of his trousers was draped around Oliver's neck. We looked on in horror as Oliver, still carrying our band mate, proceeded to negotiate his way across the motorway and weaving through the busy bank holiday traffic, he made his way towards our van.

I immediately thought how lucky it was, that the band's name was not painted on the wagon, as I hastily removed a couple of promotional posters which we had attached to the van's rear window.

I spent some great times with the Toppers, and I made lifelong friends with the boys in the band, but when Eamon Campbell decided to leave Louis Smiths Delta Boys Showband, I was asked to fill the vacant guitarist's position. As I felt that it would be a good career move for me, I agreed.

Of course this was not the end of my association with Paddy Toner, Mickey Rooney, and most of the other lads from the Toppers Showband. A year later in 1965, when the Toppers disbanded, Tommy Leddy asked me to join a new band which he was putting together from the remnants of the Toppers. He also intended to replace Oliver Mullen as manager, and to fill that role himself.

The proposed name for the new outfit was to be The Chancellors Showband, and following my very amicable exit from Louis Smith's Delta Boys in 1965, I teamed up again with my old mates under our new band name. The Chancellors turned out to be one of the most popular and successful showbands of the 1960s, and they remained in existence until the end of the decade. I will give a detailed report on my time with this band, but before I take up that story, I have a lot more unfinished business to deal with.

In order to maintain the thread of continuity, I will report on two of the previously mentioned outfits. Firstly I will complete my recollections of Dermot O'Brien and The Clubmen, and immediately follow up with a brief

The Toppers Showband:
Tommy Leddy, Gene Clinton, Willie Walsh, Johnny Milne, Tommy Moonan,
Ken Donnelly, Mal Caffrey

history of The Mountaineers.

I am well aware that a complete book could be compiled on the successful careers of many, if not all of the musicians and the outfits portrayed in this book. But as I have already indicated, my overall aim is to produce a representative snapshot of the whole era under review. Furthermore, as the book is based on my personal acquaintance with many of the musicians involved, coupled with my research of their respective outfits, each review will be a somewhat limited exercise.

Dermot O'Brien & The Clubmen:
Willie Healy, Paddy Farrell (Laytown), Reggie Lloyd, Billy O'Neill,
Denis O'Loughlin, Johnny Barton, Dermot O'Brien.

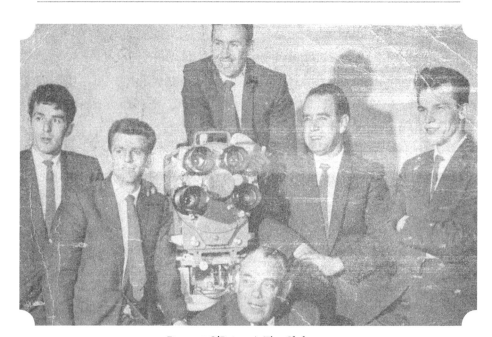

Dermot O'Brien & The Clubmen
Fintan Stanley, Johnny Barton, Dermot O'Brien, Jimmy Fitzpatrick,
Paddy Farrell, Pat Jackson.

CHAPTER TWENTY ONE

DERMOT O'BRIEN
& HIS BANDS

I n 1959 Fr. Kevin Connolly was in charge of The Lourdes Boys Club in Drogheda, and he organised a dance there every second Sunday night. Nick Smith, who was a close friend of mine and a fellow member of the C.B.S accordion band, also played with this band. Nick's family are the proprietors of the well

known N. Smith & Sons Garage on The North Road, and he is also a first cousin of The Nurse Smith's family from Mell. He left the band to follow his vocation as a Catholic Priest, and is today affectionately known as Fr. Nick.

Fr. Connolly, who was a well known G.A.A. player of that era, asked his old team mate Dermot O'Brien to fill this vacancy, and Dermot agreed, because as he said himself "I was at a loose end at that time".

The dances were very successful, and Dermot

Dermot O'Brien & The Clubmen:
Timmy Regan, Eamonn Campbell, Dermot O'Brien, Willie Healy, Derek McCormack, Tony Barrett, Johnny Barton.

Dermot O'Brien Trio: Johnny Barton, Derek McCormack, Dermot O'Brien.

persuaded Fr. Connolly to run them on a weekly basis. The band did not have a name, and so they readily accepted Fr. Connolly's suggestion of "Dermot O'Brien and The Clubmen".

The original Clubmen were mainly an all-acoustic band, and consisted of Dermot (accordion), Pat Jackson (alto sax), Tom Finglas (banjo), Jimmy Fitzpatrick (string bass) and John Donnelly (drums). This outfit remained semi-pro and continued playing music until 1962.

Dermot then decided to turn pro and formed a new professional band, but he still retained the Clubmen name. Several of the existing members of the Clubmen, with the exception of Dermot and Pat Jackson, decided against the venture into professional musicianship, and opted instead for the much safer option to "stick to the day job".

Although there were numerous personnel changes to the new band over the following years, one of the principal line-ups included Dermot, (accordion and vocals), Reggie Lloyd (bass guitar), Denis O'Loughlin, (sax/clarinet), Willie Healy, (trumpet), together with my guitar playing pals, Paddy Farrell and Eamon Campbell and Johnny Barton on drums. John Moore, another musician colleague of mine, also became a member of Dermot's band during the mid- 1960s, when he was recruited to replace Reggie Lloyd on bass guitar. (Pat Jackson had at this stage retired from The Clubmen). With his new band, Dermot's career took off in earnest and continued in a seemingly endless upward curve.

He performed extensively throughout Ireland, England, Scotland, The

Dermot O'Brien & The Clubmen:
Tom Finglas, Jimmy Fitzpatrick, Pat Jackson, Dermot O'Brien, John Donnelly.
(in the Boys' Club, Yellowbatter, Drogheda)

United states, Canada, Germany, and The United Arab Emirates. He also made top of the bill appearances at The Royal Albert Hall in London. His numerous hit singles include songs such as "The Galway Shawl", "The Old Claddagh Ring", "Spancil Hill", and his own composition of "Dublin Town In 1962". His biggest record success was without doubt "The Merry Ploughboy", which went straight to No 1 in the Irish charts. He had his own TV show which regularly topped the viewing ratings.

As well as having Drogheda man Jim Hand as his manager, his TV shows also featured regular guest appearances by the Drogheda outfit "The Mountaineers". Off Stage, Dermot was a successful arranger and producer, and he was also an accomplished song writer. Many of his songs have been recorded by other artists including Paddy Reilly, Brendan Shine, Dermot Hegarty, Bridie Gallagher, Mary McGonigle, and Daniel O'Donnell. Dermot has shared a stage with such stars

The Hayride:
Dermot O'Brien, Denis O'Loughlin, Paddy Farrell, Willie Healy, Reggie Lloyd,
Eamonn Campbell, Johnny Barton.

The Mountaineers:
Brian Hoey, Tom Finglas, Mick McGowan, Jimmy Fitzpatrick.

as Johnny Cash, Hank Snow, Bill Haley and The Comets, Buddy Herman, and he recorded a St. Patrick's Day Special with Bing Crosby in Dublin, which was shown coast to coast on The Ed Sullivan show in The United States. Dermot left his band to pursue a solo career in 2000 and continued to entertain until illness took its toll in recent times.

On closing my report on The Flying Carlton orchestra, I briefly referred to a link between two prominent members of that band and the widely acclaimed group of entertainers known as The Mountaineers. There are several reasons why I deferred my account of this outfit, and why I decided to include it following the report on Dermot O'Brien and The Clubmen. The first and principal reason is of course the personnel involved in the formation of both of these outfits. Another important reason was the close association that remained between Dermot O'Brien and The Mountaineers which was sustained over the years as their careers grew ever more successful.

The original line-up of The Mountaineers was Tom Finglas (banjo), Jimmy Fitzpatrick (bass), Brian Hoey (accordion) and Paddy Coyle (guitar). Two of the members, Jimmy Fitzpatrick and Brian Hoey, had also played with two other prominent outfits, The Flying Carlton Orchestra and Dermot O'Brien and The Clubmen, while a third member, Tom Finglas, had previously played with Dermot's band. This line-up was very often augmented by Jimmy English on violin. However, following the departure of Paddy Coyle and Jimmy English, the introduction of Mick McGowan again restored The Mountaineers to that of a four piece outfit.

The name of the outfit was derived from an American group known as The Rocky Mountaineers. They gave their debut performance at a charity concert on the opening night of The Gate Cinema in Drogheda in 1945. They were an instant success, and the news of their performance spread like wildfire. They were primarily a concert act, and it suited the group members to limit their performances to such appearances, mainly because of their commitments, initially to The Flying Carlton, and subsequently to Dermot O'Brien and The Clubmen.

The Mountaineers:
Jimmy Fitzpatrick, Mick McGowan, Tom Finglas, Eva Kierans, Brian Hoey.

Mick McGowan had already gained a wealth of experience due to his participation in variety shows such as The Drogheda Pantomime, and this experience coupled with his singing and harmonica playing allowed the group to introduce an element of comedy into their stage routines. The sight of Mick standing six feet tall and towering over Brian, who measured a mere five feet, provided them with an excellent "head start" in this regard.

In 1957 when the British Impresario, Hughie Green, came to Dublin to hold auditions for his talent show "Opportunity Knocks", the lads decided to try their hand. Hughie's show was regularly broadcast on Radio Luxemburg and had an audience of millions. It was probably the blueprint for the modern day equivalent of "The X Factor". The auditions were held in Dublin's Crystal Ballroom, and from an entry pool of 1100 hopefuls, The Mountaineers, along with four other acts, were selected to travel to London to perform at the main event. The lads put on a great performance, but unfortunately they were unsuccessful, and the competition was won by Irish vocalist Deirdre O'Callaghan.

Nevertheless, their appearance on the show greatly enhanced their reputation, and this not only led to an increase in bookings, but also led to a huge increase in audience numbers attending their performances.

They appeared in cabaret at Butlins Holiday Camp and made annual appearances at The Mary from Dungloe festival. They made frequent guest appearances on the Dublin cabaret circuit and they played at top venues such as the Green Isle Hotel and Clontarf Castle. As well as appearing on radio shows featuring Hal Roach and Kevin Hilton, they hosted their own radio show called Melody Ranch. They were regular guests on Dermot O'Brien's TV shows, and they were invited to tour with international singing star Val Doonican.

During the course of this tour, The Mountaineers were joined on stage by Irish singing star Rose Tynan. The combination was a huge success, but as Rose had her own successful career, this was to be a one-off event.

Undeterred, and as they were all agreed that a female vocalist would greatly enhance their stage performances, they approached the well known Drogheda singer Eva Kierans, and persuaded her to become a full time member of the group. Eva not only agreed, but she remained with them throughout the remainder of the band's career. Eva sang the lead vocals on the group's recording of The Old Rustic Bridge ByThe Mill, on Glenside records.

They performed this song during a concert appearance in Dublin's Capitol Cinema, and Gay Byrne, who was present in the audience, invited them to appear on his Late Late TV show. Gay must have been impressed, because he invited them back for a second appearance.

These shows were probably the highlight of the group's extraordinary career, and following many more years of playing at the top venues, Tom (The Sheriff) and the rest of his Mountaineer gang finally decided to hang up their boots.

CHAPTER TWENTY TWO

CYRIL COMES TO TOWN

I've already referred to the strong links between Dermot O'Brien and Cyril Jolley. It is probably an appropriate place in the book to give an account of Cyril's great career, not only as another internationally acclaimed accordionist, but also as a renowned band leader.

Cyril, who is a native of Dublin, began his musical career at the tender age of eight years. He trained as an accordionist at a music school in Rathmines in Dublin and his tutor was a German musician called Rosen Krantz.

At twelve years of age, he joined his brother in Birmingham in England, where he continued with his regular school studies. Whilst in Birmingham, he enrolled at the famous George Clay Music School, where he resumed his

The Cyril Jolley Group:
Gerry Hughes, Cyril Jolley, Willie Healy, Sean Donnelly

The Cyril Jolley Trio:
Ramie Smith, Paddy Farrell (Drogheda), Cyril Jolley

The Cyril Jolley Group:
Sean Reynolds, Gerry Hughes, Sean Donnelly, Cyril Jolley

music studies. It was during his time at this college that he made the journey to London in 1950 to take part in the all England accordion championships, and as already mentioned, he was awarded the title of English Champion accordionist in the under sixteen division at the festival.

He returned to Ireland in 1951 where he met with Peadar Smith who invited him to his home in Mell to meet his mother The Nurse, and this in turn led to his long time association with Dermot O'Brien.

Cyril and Dermot began rehearsing as an accordion duo, and in 1952 they performed on several variety shows which included an appearance on the Drogheda Pantomime. Dermot then spent some time playing accordion with The Vincent Lowe Trio, while Cyril filled a similar role with The Jackie Hearst Trio. However, during this period they continued to perform as a duo at the occasional concert.

In 1955 when Scottish accordionist Jimmy Shand and his band had a major hit with their recording of The Bluebell Polka, both Dermot and Cyril agreed that the time was ripe for them to form their own Ceili band. Later that year they launched The St. Malachys Ceili Band, and they were an instant hit. They continued to perform successfully for several more years, and the line-up, which remained unchanged throughout, included Dermot, Cyril, Brian Lynch (fiddle), Phyllis McKenny (piano), Sean O'Brien (drums), and Jimmy Walpole (double bass). Also during this period, Cyril regularly joined forces with Raimie Smith (drums), and Dessie McManus (keyboards). This outfit was known as The Galanto Trio.

Following the demise of The St Malachys Ceili Band in 1958/59, Dermot began his long term association with the Clubmen, and Cyril travelled to London to continue with his music studies. At the end of a four year music study course, Cyril was appointed as Principle of The Hohner Accordion College in Dublin in 1963. This new position was indeed a very prestigious one, and one of his principal duties was to demonstrate the new Hohner Cordovox.

Nevertheless, Cyril's love of performing live on stage with other musicians soon led to him forming yet another outfit and taking to the road again. In 1963 he enlisted the services of Ramie Smith (Drums), and Ralph Lynch (Double Bass), and together they became known as The Cyril Jolley Trio. This group had a long and successful innings. They generally performed at weddings and reunions, but the majority of their gigs were at The Fairways Hotel in Dundalk where they were retained as the hotel's resident group.

Over the years, and indeed right up to the present time, Cyril has been the front man in a succession of fine bands and has always succeeded in surrounding himself with many of the finest musicians from this area. Apart from those already mentioned, the following is a small selection of the many other musicians who played in Cyril's bands: Gerry Hughes (Drums), Willie Healy (Trumpet), Tony Barrett (Trumpet), the two guitarists of the same name, Paddy Farrell (Greenlanes), Paddy Farrell (Laytown), Shaun Reynolds (Guitar and vocals), and Timmy Regan (Guitar and vocals).

Without doubt, this section would not be complete without the inclusion of a detailed report on the wonderful career of a third local accordionist who not only went on to achieve international acclaim, but who also had close links to both Dermot O'Brien and Cyril Jolley. I refer of course to Fintan Stanley, the maestro from Clogherhead.

CHAPTER TWENTY THREE

EL RELICARIO
& FINTAN STANLEY

During my accordion playing days in 1960, I was invited to perform at a Sunday night concert in the parish hall in Dunleer, Co. Louth. The duration of my solo performance lasted about twenty minutes, and my play list for the show included a Spanish tune called "El Relicario". One of the other acts on the show that night was another solo accordionist called Fintan Stanley.

Although I had already known Fintan, we were not very well acquainted. However, on the following night he paid me a visit at my home in Mell, and as he had brought his accordion with him, he asked if it would be ok for him to bring it into my house. I agreed of course.

He told me that he had listened to my performance on the previous night, and he particularly liked my rendition of El Relicario. When he asked if I would play this tune for him, I duly obliged. He then asked if I would play it again, which I also did. On hearing it for the second time, he said "That's ok, I think I have it".

Not only was this quite a difficult piece to play, but I had specially adapted it to suit myself. I had also spent two weeks rehearsing it before I was satisfied with my performance. So I said to him ok let's hear you play it. He then proceeded to give a virtuoso performance of the tune.

It could be construed that he already knew how to play it, but as he played it very closely to my own personal interpretation, I'm fairly certain that this was indeed his first performance of the tune. My belief then, that he is indeed a very special musician, has since been borne out in spades, and can be seen in the following report on his rise to fame.

Fintan was just twelve years of age when he acquired his first accordion, a single row button key instrument, and he took to playing it almost immediately. It wasn't long before he upgraded to a double row accordion and quickly gained a reputation for his playing skills. I should mention here that I played a piano key accordion, and for the benefit of those readers who may be unfamiliar with the difference between both instruments, they each require very differing playing skills.

Our careers paths crossed again when he appeared on the Radio Eireann show "Children at the Microphone", because some time later, I played my accordion on that same show. He was runner up in the All Ireland Accordion Championships at his first attempt, and the following year, at the age of 14, he was crowned All Ireland Champion. When he was 15 years of age, he played with The Gallowglass Ceili Band, and around the same time he also played with Dermot O'Brien and his Ceili band. He later played with Dermot and The Clubmen.

His career took a different course when he signed on with ocean liners and cargo ships and he spent the next few years travelling the globe. He returned to Ireland in the late 1950s and rejoined the Gallowglass Ceili Band. The Showband craze was taking hold across Ireland at that time and as the Gallowglass and their style of music was still in great demand abroad, they spent much of this period playing at venues in Britain and The United States.

One of the many highlights in Fintan's career must surely be the great reception he received for his performance at New York's Carnegie Hall. He returned to Ireland in the mid 1960s where he met and married Maisie McDaniels. Maisie was one of Ireland's top female vocalists of that era.

During my time with The Chancellors Showband, we played on a variety concert in Drogheda's Gate Cinema and Maisie together with Fintan appeared on the same show. The couple continued to perform in cabaret and television, before returning to Sligo where they formed a band called The Nashville Ramblers. Fintan later returned to America where he resumed his career as a solo accordionist and singer.

He now spends most of his time performing at venues along the east coast of the U.S. Occasionally, he still returns to Ireland to perform, and he usually includes some local venues on any such visits.

The Chancellors Reunion:
Harry O'Reilly (author), John (Twick) Donnelly, Tommy Leddy, Tony Cassidy, Mickey Rooney, Frankie Smith.

CHAPTER TWENTY FOUR

EARLY GUITAR-PLAYING DAYS

following my exit from the Toppers Showband, and before I joined Louis Smith's Delta Boys, I formed what is generally known as a Garage Band with a few of my former school friends in 1964. It was an all guitar outfit consisting of Tony Cassidy, Raymond Green and me. We rehearsed in Raymond's garage in Mell. We were occasionally joined by Pat Fitzpatrick on bass guitar. The band was not special of itself, but the personal friendships and the musical careers of the individuals concerned, were to be maintained for many future years.

Our one and only gig was at a talent contest for up and coming young pop groups, and was held in Ardee, Co. Louth. For the purpose of the competition we needed a group name and a drummer. As I recall, we called ourselves The Heat Beats, and we recruited another school friend called Pat Fox to be our drummer for the occasion. The venue was a field outside the town, and the performance area was the back end of an articulated truck, parked in the middle of the field. I don't recall the judge's verdict, but I'm fairly sure we were not among the winners.

However, not only was this event relevant to our future careers, but we became long time friends with the members of another group from Bettystown who also took part in that same contest. This group were called The Road Runners, and featured Phil (Birch) McLoughlin on lead guitar. These guys went on to carve out a long and hugely successful career in entertainment.

Despite numerous personnel changes, and indeed, several alterations to the name of the group, I have, with Phil's assistance, put together a brief history of their progression over the years.

The group emerged from a collection of school friends who used to while

The Roadrunners:
Phil (Birch) McLoughlin, Robert Berney, Leontia Somers,
Mick McLoughlin, John Somers.

away the cold winter nights in the seaside village of Bettystown by holding musical evenings in a house at the rear of the Somers family shop in the village square. The group included the McLoughlin brothers Mick and Phil, together with Leontia Somers (vocalist), John Somers (guitar), and Bob Berney (bass). The group's guitarists were ably assisted by the great Paddy Farrell, whose career I have already recorded in some detail.

Following lots of practice, and the compilation of a small repertoire, they decided to seek an outlet for their new found talents. Of course the main obstacle to making their debut performance was a complete lack of any P.A. system. To overcome this, they enlisted the assistance of a mutual friend called Gerry Wickham, who was at that time the manager of a top recording outfit known as The Graduates Showband. Gerry gave them a regular half hour slot playing support to his band at the Pavilion Ballroom in Skerries, Co. Dublin. This opportunity not only provided them with the chance to play before huge audiences, but they also got to use the band's top of the range instruments and

P.A. system.

The experience stood them in good stead, and gave them the confidence to obtain their own modest P.A. system, and to seek bookings in their own right. The electrical skills of bass guitarist Bob Berney proved invaluable in this respect, when he not only constructed two of the group's amplifiers, but he also built his own bass guitar. Finally, when the Laytown and Bettystown Golf Club engaged them for the club's summer season of dances, they were on their way.

As these dances were quite lengthy affairs, the Road Runners decided to follow Gerry Wickham's example, and they in turn secured the services of another up and coming outfit to play a support role for their dances.

The personnel of this as yet unnamed outfit would have an important impact on the future of The Road Runners, and it is with this in mind, that I have included details of their line-up. They were Niall Corrigan, Dave Gibney, John Gogarty, Shaun Black, and a certain Mr Neil Jordan. This was the internationally acclaimed film producer, whose family spent their summer holidays in Bettystown and as he had become friendly with the lads he began playing guitar on stage with them.

Of course, as it was only a summer gig, he didn't stay very long with them before deciding that his future career lay elsewhere.

In the mid-1960s, when Bob Berney left the group, he was replaced by a school pal of the remaining members called Paul (Cisco) O'Kane. Although Cisco was highly regarded as a piano player, he agreed to fill the group's bass guitarist vacancy.

The group continued with this format until they decided to call it a day, and to bring to an end the very successful four year career of The Road Runners. There are a few other outfits with connections to The Road Runners, but the main link to each of them is that they all had Phil McLoughlin as their lead guitarist.

I intend to deal with each of them in turn, but yet again, in the interest of continuity, and because I am still dealing with outfits from the 1960s, I will

The Trolls:
Niall Corrigan , Mo Conlon, Shaun Black, Mick Doherty, Birch McLoughlin.

complete this section with a review of the immediate successors to the Road Runners, namely The Trolls.

Following the disbandment of the Road Runners, the previously mentioned group who had been playing relief work for The Road Runners, also decided to call it a day, and the subsequent disbandment of both groups led to the formation of a new group called The Trolls.

Two of the Road Runners, Phil and Cisco, were joined by Shaun Black and Niall Corrigan from the other group, and as Shaun and Niall's group had by now been using the name of The Trolls, they all agreed to assume this name for the newly formed group. The new line-up consisted of Phil McLoughlin (lead guitar), Cisco O'Kane (bass guitar), Niall Corrigan (rhythm guitar), and Shaun Black (drums).

They continued to play to capacity audiences at The Laytown and Bettystown Golf Club gigs, and at the Friday night gigs at The Parochial Hall in Laytown. It was during this period, 1967/1968, when The Golf Club Committee decided to alternate their weekend gigs between our band The Chancellors and The Trolls that our paths were to cross again.

I must add that The Golf Club gig was without doubt, the leading venue in the North East of the country during the mid to late 1960s. When bass guitarist Cisco O'Kane decided to leave the group, he was succeeded by Tom Reilly, and Tom in turn was succeeded by Mo Conlon. It was around this time that the group became a regular attraction at the Saturday night gigs at the Drogheda Rugby Club dances on Ballymakenny Road.

In the early 1970s The Trolls took the decision to disband and to re-group, and as I have already mentioned, Phil McLoughlin remained at the core of this new group and indeed of several other groups to subsequently emerge from the demise of The Trolls. I have included the details of these groups in the final part of the book.

The Delta Boys:
Louis Smith, Eamonn Campbell, Syd Kierans, Pal McDonnell,
John Leonard, John (Twick) Donnelly, Terry Smith, (The Abbey Ballroom)

Louis Smith Dance Band:
Back: Ben Mullen, Charlie McEnteggart. Front: Larry Moroney, Ray Buckley,
Louis Smith, Christy Smith, Terry Smith, Gerry (Oscar) Traynor.

CHAPTER TWENTY FIVE

THE BEGINNING OF THE 60S

I will now return to the early 1960s, and continue to report on the musicians, bands, and events, during what was indeed a very special decade.

Irish showbands generally played the popular music of the day, and with groups such as The Beatles and The Rolling Stones dominating the record charts, the variety of songs to include in our repertoire was fantastic.

From my point of view, it was a great time to be a guitar playing teenager and to have the opportunity to play such great music with some very popular bands.

My guitar playing improved quite considerably during the period I spent playing with Louis Smith and The Delta Boys. This was due in no small part to the guidance I received from the great man himself.

Louis enjoyed a long and illustrious musical career. He was renowned throughout the country, not only for his leadership of some of Ireland's greatest bands, but also for his gifted musical ability and his overall dedication to music itself.

When Louis' family arrived in Drogheda in the late 1940s, he was already an accomplished piano player, and following his enrolment in the local C.B.S., he secured a position with Pat Jackson and his orchestra.

During his time with Pat, he also played piano with some of the other local bands. In 1955, following his exit from Pat's orchestra, he formed the first of several of his own bands. As with all of Louis' Bands, his brother Terry invariably played Tenor saxophone.

Together with Louis and Terry, one of the band's earliest line-ups also included Ben Mullen (alto sax), Raymond Buckey (alto sax), Frank Quinn (trumpet), Tim Hughes (vocalist) & Gerry (Oscar) Traynor (drums).

Louis Smith (Opening of the Palm Court Ballroom) :
Terry Smith, Ben Mullen, Christy Smith, Louis Smith.

Following the departures of Tim Hughes and Frank Quinn, Ralph Lynch took over the role of vocalist, and Christy Smith replaced Frank Quinn on trumpet. When Ralph was later recruited by The Flying Carlton, Louis decided to make some further changes in personnel.

The line-up that took to the stage on the opening night of The Palm Court Ballroom, in the White Horse Hotel in Drogheda, included Louis, Terry, Ben Mullen, John Hanratty, Christy Smith, Charlie McEnteggart, Larry Moroney, and Gerry Traynor. Yet another change to this line-up took place when Charlie McEnteggart left the band and was replaced by Owen Lynch (brother of Ralph).

The end of the 1950s, and the commencement of the 1960s, was a time of great change on the band scene. Not only was the music changing in style, but The Showband phenomenon was just beginning to take hold.

These are two of the main reasons put forward to account for the sudden rush of musicians, not only changing bands, but eagerly joining many of the

The Louis Smith Dance Band:
Terry Smith, Gerry (Oscar) Traynor, Owen Lynch. John Hanratty, Paddy Farrell
(Laytown), Louis Smith, Larry Moroney, Christy Smith

newly formed outfits. Furthermore, many musicians threw caution to the wind, and gave up their jobs to pursue a full time career in music.

In order to keep track of the various movements of personnel during this period, and while still trying to avoid the tendency to end up with a book more akin to a telephone directory, I hope that the photographs I have included will be of some assistance in this regard.

One of these photographs includes the line-up of The Louis Smith Band, shortly before Louis decided to change the name of his band to that of The Delta Boys Showband.

During the lifetime of The Delta Boys, there were several different line-ups, and in order to simplify matters, I will document the makeup of each one individually.

Line-up number one of The Delta Boys Showband was Louis, Terry, Christy Smith (trumpet), Paddy Farrell (Laytown) (lead guitar), Patsy Carton (rhythm guitar), Gerry Saurin (bass guitar) and Mickey Traynor (drums).

The Louis Smith Orchestra:

Gerry (Oscar) Traynor, Charley McEnteggart, Terry Smith, Ben Mullen, Ray Buckley, Tim Hughes, Frank Quinn, Louis Smith.

In the second line-up, Christy Smith and Mickey Traynor were replaced by Syd Kierans (trumpet), and John (Twick) Donnelly (drums).

In the third line-up, Patsy Carton and Gerry Saurin were replaced by Eamonn Campbell (guitar), and Pal McDonnell (bass guitar).

In the fourth line-up, Paddy Farrell was replaced by vocalist John Leonard.

I was recruited to replace Eamonn Campbell, who together with John (Twick) Donnelly and John Leonard, had all decided to become part of the newly formed group known as The Bee Vee Five.

Following the departure of this trio, the fifth line-up of The Delta Boys consisted of Louis, Terry, Syd Kierans, Bruce Moran (drums), Mickey Black (vocals), John Moore (rhythm guitar) and myself (lead guitar). There was just one further change to the band's line-up, and it involved the recruitment of Maurice Downey as my replacement on lead guitar in mid-1965.

Following a marathon series of changes to his band's line-ups, Louis decided to return to a more sedate lifestyle, where he played a lot of solo gigs and small events.

This of course was not to be the last of Louis and his bands, because late 1968 would see him bring together many of his former band mates, and he returned in style with his new version of The Louis Smith Big Band.

As this event occurred near the end of the 1960s decade, and as there were simply so many musicians involved, I will include my account of The Big Band in the third and final section of this book.

****

The formation of the fifth and final line-up of The Delta Boys was brought about by the departure of three of its previous members, John Leonard, Eamonn Campbell, and John (Twick) Donnelly, who had been persuaded to become part of a new 1960s group called the Bee Vee Five. This seems like an appropriate place to document the career of this outfit.

Having been advised of the potential benefits of creating and promoting

The Louis Smith Orchestra:
Terry Smith, John Hanratty, Gerry (Oscar) Traynor, (drums), Ben Mullen, Larry
Moroney, Owen Lynch (double bass), Christy Smith, Louis Smith.

his own band in those heady days of the mid 1960s, Drogheda businessman
Bernard V. Anderson decided to embark on just such a venture.

Bernard quite liked the idea of being associated with a top musical group
bearing his name and he quickly set about enticing some of the top musicians
of the day to join his new band.

He initially approached Erroll Sweeney about the project. Erroll in turn
invited four other musicians to accompany him in the venture. Three of these
musicians were former members of the Delta Boys Show Band, and, initially,
Tom Sullivan was meant to be the fifth member of the group. However, after a
brief spell Tom decided to move on and was replaced by Gerry Saurin.

As Gerry was also a former member of The Delta Boys Showband, the
creation of The Bee Vee Five had a significant impact on the membership of
Louis Smith's Band.

When Bernard finally launched his new outfit under the banner of The Bee
Vee Five, the line-up consisted of John Leonard (vocals), Eamonn Campbell

Louis Smith (Opening of the Palm Court Ballroom):
Ben Mullen, Larry Moroney.

(lead guitar), Erroll Sweeney (rhythm guitar), Gerry Saurin (bass guitar) and John (Twick) Donnelly (drums). Bernard ensured that his group took to the road equipped, not only with the very best in P. A. sound systems, but he also provided them with some top of the range musical instruments.

The Bee Vee Five were an excellent outfit with a significant fan base, but their existence was rather short lived. Not only did the group disband after approximately one year, but half way through that period they endured a significant change in personnel when three of the original members decided to exit the group and pursue their careers elsewhere.

Eamonn Campbell joined Dermot O'Brien and the Clubmen, Twick Donnelly joined Dublin based The Odeon Show band, and John Leonard embarked on his own career, part of which I have already detailed.

The second and final line-up of The Bee Vee Five was Erroll Sweeney (rhythm guitar), Gerry Saurin (bass guitar), Jon Ledingham (drums), Patsy Carton (lead guitar) and Brian Trench (piano). Patsy Carton was also a former

The Delta Boys Showband:
Louis Smith, Mickey Black, John Moore, Terry Smith, Maurice Downey,
Bruce Moran, Syd Kierans

The Bee Vee Five:
Erroll Sweeney, Brian Trench, Jon Ledingham, Patsy Carton, Gerry Saurin.

member of The Delta Boys Showband.

The inclusion of a piano into the Bee Vee Five's second line-up greatly restricted their appearances. This was mainly because of the scarcity of venues where a piano was provided for visiting entertainers during the 1960s. Consequently, during their short career, the majority of their gigs were held in hotels which catered for reunions, weddings, and college events.

One interesting aspect of the group's break up was the excitement which the sale of their very expensive equipment created amongst the local musicians. News of the great bargains to be had spread like wildfire and there was a major scramble to be first in the queue.

Following the demise of The Bee Vee Five, Erroll Sweeney followed a career which would eventually lead to him teaming up again with John Leonard. Gerry Saurin decided to call it a day, Brian Trench resumed his university education, Jon Ledingham embarked on a solo recording career, and Patsy Carton also resumed his university education.

When Patsy qualified as a school teacher, he formed his own part time musical group, and he continues to perform with them.

The Bee Vee Five:
Brian Trench, Jon Ledingham, Gerry Saurin, Patsy Carton, Erroll Sweeney.

The Bee Vee Five:
John Leonard, Tom Sullivan, John (Twick) Donnelly, Erroll Sweeney,
Eamonn Campbell. (original line-up)

CHAPTER TWENTY SIX

FROM TOPPERS TO CHANCELLORS

During the month of May 1965, as previously mentioned, I received a visit from Tommy Leddy regarding his intention to create a new Showband from the remains of the disbanded Toppers Showband. As I was still a member of The Delta Boys Showband, I insisted on giving Louis Smith a few weeks' notice prior to my departure from his band. This was agreed, and Tommy set about preparing for the launch of our new band.

I finished playing with The Delta Boys in mid-June and I arranged to meet up with Tommy and the other musicians for our first rehearsal during the first week of July 1965.

The Chancellors Showband was originally a seven piece outfit, and consisted of five former members of The Toppers Showband, together with two new recruits.

The former Toppers members were Tommy Leddy (bass guitar), Mickey Rooney (vocalist), Paddy Toner (drums), Frankie Smith (trumpet) and I took on the role of lead guitarist.

The two new recruits were John Moore (rhythm guitar), and Ernie McCarthy (tenor saxophone). John Moore had previously played with me in The Delta Boys Showband, and Ernie had been a member of The Hi Lows Showband from his home town of Longford, prior to his arrival in Drogheda. The choice of the name for the new band was most definitely decided by Tommy Leddy. The rest of us had some misgivings about the name sounding uncomfortably close to that of "Chancers", and we put forward several alternatives, but to no avail. Tommy was determined to adopt the name of The

PRESENTATION CONVENT, GREENHILLS

INVITES

....

TO THEIR
SHROVE DANCE
AT
PALM COURT, WHITE HORSE HOTEL
TUESDAY, 18th. FEBRUARY. '69.
MUSIC BY:
-- THE CHANCELLORS --
DANCING 8-12 ADM. 5/- (BY INVITATION ONLY

The Chancellors' Ticket

Chancellors, and he could be very persuasive when he set his mind on something. He successfully convinced us that his choice of The Chancellors would act as a spur for the band to become so good that we would soon rise above any such jibes that might be thrown our way. Not for the first time Tommy got his way.

The venue we chose for our rehearsals was an old army Nissen-Hut, which had been converted to a communal meeting hall. It was situated on The Donore Road, just outside Drogheda, and the caretaker was a certain Mrs White who lived in an adjoining house. We paid her a weekly rental fee for the use of "The Hut", and we continued to avail of this facility during the next few years.

Most of us had the experience of performing together regularly during the previous few years, and so we had a ready-made dance programme. Having experienced the drudgery of long distance travel to and from gigs, we decided from the outset to curtail our travelling to within a seventy mile radius of Drogheda. As most of the major towns and dance venues were within this catchment area, and as we were also quite familiar with dance promoters etc., we found it rather easy to obtain such bookings.

And so, with the addition of a few newly rehearsed songs to our already comprehensive repertoire, and with several advance bookings in our diary, The Chancellors took to the road during the month of July 1965.

Most of our early gigs were at venues where we had previously played, but as we grew in popularity, we also acquired a significant fan base. This in turn

The Chancellors' Poster

led to an increase in bookings, and we began to make appearances at an ever increasing number of new venues.

I will of course give a sample insight into life on the road with The Chancellors, but before I do, I must deal with a matter concerning the personnel position within the band.

There was just one change of personnel to the original line-up during the lifetime of The Chancellors Showband, and this occurred within the first few months of its formation in 1965. John Moore accepted an offer to join Dermot O'Brien and The Clubmen as a full time musician, and I encouraged my old

The Chancellors Showband
Tommy Leddy, Paddy Toner, Ernie McCarthy, Tony Cassidy, Frankie Smith,
Harry O'Reilly, Mickey Rooney.

friend Tony Cassidy, to fill the vacant position of rhythm guitarist with our band.

Our first gig with The Chancellors Showband took place within a week or so of the band's formation. Following a series of rehearsals, which left us ready for our first assignment, we set off on what was a warm and sultry Sunday afternoon in late July of 1965. The dance venue was a large marquee somewhere in County Longford. The use of a marquee as a temporary dance venue was quite common during the 50s and 60s. They were generally rented out by rural parish committees and were used as the central meeting place for whatever fete or fundraising event the committee wished to facilitate.

These parochial venues always attracted large audiences and this night was no exception. It was usual for the dances to last for up to four hours, so we normally took a break half way through such nights. In order not to interrupt the musical entertainment, we used a format whereby four band members took their break, whilst the remaining three carried on playing. The punters

The Chancellors Showband:
Ernie McCarthy, John Moore, Tommy Leddy, Paddy Toner, Frankie Smith,
Mickey Rooney, Harry O'Reilly (Author).

generally knew what to expect and would mostly sit these dances out.

The marquee was usually erected in some local farmer's field, and as this was long before the provision of a portaloo, the only toilet facility available at this particular venue, was a primitive hole in the ground. This was also the night that we were wearing our new swish band uniforms which were light blue in colour. Our vocalist, Mickey Rooney, was in the habit of wearing braces on his trousers, and on this occasion when he decided to use the toilet, he had to remove his nice blue uniform jacket, which he placed on the ground beside him. When the four members made their way back to the stage through the seated audience Frankie Smith, our trumpet player, let out a roar, "what is that awful smell", quickly followed by, "Jesus, look at Mickey's coat". The back of Mickey's blue coat was by now distinctly brown. The coat was hastily thrown outside the rear of the marquee, and we were able to resume playing music. We returned home that evening with the soiled coat hanging from the roof rack of the band wagon.

The Chancellors Showband:
Frankie Smith, Tommy Leddy, Mickey Rooney, Harry O'Reilly (Author),
Tony Cassidy, Paddy Toner, Ernie McCarthy.

The Chancellors Showband:
Tommy Leddy, John Moore, Paddy Toner, Frankie Smith, Mickey Rooney,
Ernie McCarthy, Harry O'Reilly (Author).

Now Mickey had a very pronounced, almost arrogant stride whenever he approached a bandstand, and as I sat inside the van on our homeward journey, I grew ever more mortified as I pondered what must have gone through the minds of the seated masses in the marquee.

However, the following weekend, Mickey showed up with the coat in pretty good order. We asked how he managed to get it cleaned, and he told us that he had left it into the local dry cleaners. He also added that, when he collected it from the cleaners, there was a warning note attached which read "In future, if you require any garments of a similar nature to be cleaned by us, we will require at least two weeks' notice".

The Rink in Aungier Street in Dublin was a well established and very popular night club where many of the up and coming rock and pop groups of the 1960s appeared. It was also one of the new venues where The Chancellors were booked to play, and following our first appearance there, we were offered as many return bookings as we could handle. This venue became an important milestone in the career of the band. As we were the only showband appearing at The Rink, we found ourselves competing with some of the leading rock and pop outfits in the country. I believe that this helped to improve, and to influence the musical direction of the band for the remainder of the 1960s.

The Rink, as its name suggests, was formerly a skating rink, which had been converted to a dance venue. The proprietor was a gentleman known as Solomon (Solly) White, and he took an immediate shine to our band, so much so that he wanted to be our manager. We did not encourage him in this regard, but when he produced a bottle of whiskey, the mood became more amiable. While we persuaded him that we were quite happy with our own managerial arrangements, we agreed to his suggestion of appearing at The Rink on a weekly basis. As I recall, the meeting ended quite cordially.

However, my recollection of this meeting, also brought to mind another incident which took place on the night, and that was the vision of Mickey holding out his drinks glass while Solly poured some more whiskey into it, and Solly saying in an increasingly agitated voice "Mickey, say when, please say when".

Solly told us that his favourite song was "Back to Sorrento", and he would like to hear Mickey sing it for him. Although this song was not part of our repertoire, we promised to rehearse it, and to play it for him at a later date.

We produced what we felt was a very fine arrangement of the song, and although Solly loved it, I think our effort was rather lost on the young audience who usually attended The Rink. Later that night I was handed a note from someone in the audience which read, please play again that lovely song called "Back to Toronto".

Our regular appearances at The Rink began to attract very large audiences, and this in turn brought us to the attention of many other promoters in the Dublin area. Although we did not set out to make so many appearances in and around Dublin, by accepting such bookings, we inevitably found ourselves playing more and more along the east coast of Ireland, to the virtual exclusion of dance venues situated elsewhere. Nevertheless, the new travel arrangements brought a welcome relief from the drudgery of spending several hours travelling to a gig in the back of an overcrowded band wagon

CHAPTER TWENTY SEVEN

OUR GIG AT THE CASTLE

In 1967 The Chancellors were on the crest of the wave, and they were set fair to continue in great demand for the remainder of the 1960s. In order to give a final flavour of this great era of dance music, and to give an insight into some of the great guys who provided that music, I have decided to mark the end of this section by including a few more anecdotes from our life on the road with The Chancellors.

One of our most successful and memorable gigs took place at Slane Castle in May of 1967, and I have decided to include a detailed account of the events surrounding the occasion.

Mickey had been acquainted with a butler at Slane Castle in Co Meath, and as this gentleman was also aware that Mickey was lead vocalist with our band, he made enquiries about our availability to perform at a birthday celebration which was due to take place at The Castle. Mickey passed on the details to our manager Tommy Leddy, who confirmed the booking with Lady Eileen Mountcharles. The event was to celebrate her son's 16th birthday, and as far as we were concerned, it was just another booking engagement.

When we arrived at the castle, we soon realised that this gig was going to be quite an extraordinary event. The butler met us outside the castle and escorted us to the ballroom, where we were greeted with a welcoming drink.
Everything about the performance area was breathtaking, and not at all what we were expecting. The lighting and decor was fabulous, and the lads thought they had just arrived in heaven, when they realised that the ballroom area was surrounded by a selection of self-service wine and spirits bars.

When we had assembled our gear, and carried out our sound checks, the butler invited us to dinner. However, as he led us down stairs to the servants' quarters, we soon realised that the hospitality to share the same meal as the guests did not stretch to actually dining with them. Nevertheless, we were treated with the utmost courtesy, and we were served the same celebratory meal, simultaneously as it was being served upstairs.

Suitably wined and dined, we returned to the reception area, carried out a final sound check and prepared for action.

When we looked for Mickey, we noticed that he had already made himself very much at home. He approached the stage area with a drink in one hand, and the other resting on the shoulder of the birthday boy himself. Mickey then invited us to meet his new found friend, who he introduced as Viscount Slane. We offered our congratulations and following the usual pleasantries, we got the show underway.

The band received a tremendous reception from the guests, who all agreed that the whole affair was an unqualified success. We received numerous encores, and following the offer of a considerable financial incentive, we were persuaded to continue playing for a further hour.

While we were packing up our gear, Lady Eileen enquired about our availability regarding a return gig, and almost with one voice we all replied, "when is it". It turned out that the gig was scheduled for a few weeks later, and to our great disappointment, it did not involve a return visit to The Castle, but was due to be held in The Royal Hibernian Hotel in Dublin. We did receive and accept the offer of this gig. I don't remember the details surrounding the occasion, but I do recall that it was organised for Lord Henry and a group of his pals, and that this evening also turned out to be a great success.

As we were generally regarded as a 1960s pop band, and in the light of subsequent events surrounding Slane Castle and its world famous concerts, it is nice to think that we can lay a very small claim to having played there before U2 and The Stones etc.

CHAPTER TWENTY EIGHT

YOUNG GUNS BREAK AWAY

In my review of Eamonn Campbell's career, I referred to a new showband called The Tigermen formed in May 1968, and evolved from the dissolution of the partnership between Dermot O'Brien and The Clubmen.

Dermot decided to pursue his own solo career, and The Clubmen, following several weeks of intense rehearsals, made their debut at The Arcadia in Cork City on Easter Sunday 1968. However, due to a dispute regarding the use of the name "The Clubmen", the band found it necessary to choose another name, and The Tigermen was the preferred option. The band also chose to project a greater pop image for their supporters, and to this end they decided to feature Timmy Regan as their lead vocalist and front man.

The Tigermen Showband: Johnny Barton, Willie Healy, Eamonn Campbell, Timmy Regan, Jim Newman, Kenny Doyle, Denis O'Loughlin.

The Tigermen Showband:
Kenny Doyle, Eamonn Campbell, Timmy Regan,
Robin Taylor, Willie Healy, Johnny Barton, Gerry Hughes.

Timmy, who is originally from Cork City, first came to the attention of Dermot O'Brien at a gig in City Hall in Cork. Timmy was lead vocalist with the support band for Dermot and The Clubmen at the gig, and Dermot was so impressed with Timmy's performance that he invited him to join his band as lead vocalist. Timmy at first decided to complete his studies in Cork, and some months later he moved to Drogheda and accepted Dermot's invitation.

The line-up for the new band consisted of Timmy (vocalist), Johnny Barton (drums), Willie Healy (trumpet), Eamonn Campbell (lead guitar), Denis O'Loughlin (saxophone), Jimmy Newman (bass guitar), and Kenny Doyle (keyboards). The Tigermen enjoyed a very successful career during the remainder of 1968 and throughout 1969 but like so many other showbands, there were several changes in personnel during their existence.

Most of these changes took place during the first six months of the bands existence. The first band member to move on was Jim Newman. Jim was replaced

The Tigermen Showband:
Willie Healy, Timmy Regan, Paddy Farrell (Laytown), Eamonn Campbell, Kenny Doyle, Tony Barrett, Johnny Barton.

on bass guitar by Ollie Bird, who in turn was replaced by Gerry Hughes. The second change took place with the departure of Denis O'Louglin. Denis was replaced on saxophone by Clarrie Daniels, who in turn was replaced by Tony Kierans. A few months later when saxophone player Tony Kierans also decided to move on, he was replaced by Tony Barrett on trumpet. This latest change in personnel created a new sound for the band as they now featured two trumpeters, Willie Healy and Tony Barrett, in their brass section. Finally, in the latter half of 1969, when Gerry Hughes decided to exit the band, he was replaced by Paddy Farrell (Laytown).

As I have already reported, Paddy had previously been lead guitarist with The Clubmen, but, as the vacancy was for a bass guitarist, he was happy to accept that position and to rejoin his former band mates. This was to be the line-up of The Tigermen until late 1969, when the decision was taken to dispense with their Showband image and to regroup as a big band with a new name and a new image.

During their successful run, The Tigermen built up an extensive fan base and

The Jubilee Orchestra:
Kevin O'Brien, Ray Buckley, Ben Mullen, Eamonn Campbell, Derek McCormack, Jimmy Creavney, Willie Healy, Tony Barrett, Timmy Regan, Johnny Barton.

regularly played to huge audiences. They also produced three excellent records. The first of these was called "Old Time Movies", and was released in late 1968. The record, which featured Timmy on vocals, received extensive air play, and succeeded in reaching the number three spot on the Irish charts. Their second recording also featured Timmy and was entitled "Sweet Dreams". Their third recording entitled "Waltzing On Top Of The World" was released following the return of Paddy Farrell and, in order to showcase the versatility of the band, they took the decision to feature Paddy on vocals.

The decision to disband The Tigermen Showband, and to reform as an orchestra, was influenced by the success of several other big bands which were performing throughout the country at that time. The name chosen for this new outfit was The Jubilee Orchestra, and they hoped to occupy a position in what was considered to be a niche market. Paddy Farrell declined the offer of a position in this new venture, and Derek McCormack was chosen as his replacement. The line-up was augmented by three other Drogheda based musicians, Ben Mullen, Ray Buckley, and Kevin O'Brien, and the band was launched in The Arcadia Ballroom in Cork City at the beginning of 1970. However the venture turned out to be a rather brief affair, and although they enjoyed considerable success during their tenure, the decision to disband The Jubilee Orchestra was taken in the latter half of 1970.

The dissolution of the big band coincided with a re-forming of Dermot O'Brien and The Clubmen, and the new six piece line-up consisted of Dermot, Timmy Regan, Eamonn Campbell, Derek McCormack, Tony Barrett and Johnny Barton. This particular version of The Clubmen had a wonderful career, and continued with the same personnel until the end of 1972. With the departure of Timmy Regan and Tony Barrett in late December 1972, followed by the subsequent departure of Eamonn Campbell in 1973, Dermot O'Brien took the decision to continue as a three-piece outfit. The new line-up became known as The Dermot O'Brien Trio, consisted of Dermot with Johnny Barton (drums) and Derek McCormack (guitar). This particular outfit enjoyed an extraordinary globe-trotting career, and the personnel remained unchanged until 1982, when Dermot O'Brien decided to disband the group and to pursue his career as a solo artiste.

The Tigermen Showband:
Denis O'Loughlin, Willie Healy, Johnny Barton, Timmy Regan, Jim Newman,
Kenny Doyle, Eamonn Campbell.

Johnny Barton in Dubai on tour with Dermot O'Brien in the Middle East

CHAPTER TWENTY NINE

DEREK COMES INTO HIS OWN

following the dissolution of The Dermot O'Brien Trio, Johnny Barton took the decision to retire as a professional musician, but Derek McCormack's career took off in spectacular fashion, and I have included a brief profile of Derek's glittering career in the following article.

Derek was indeed destined for a life of show business. His mother Marie McCormack (nee Martin) was a member of the famous Martin Show, and together with her brother Harry Martin, they included Derek in several of their many stage shows at the tender age of just ten years. Derek's brother Roy also appeared regularly with The Martin Show, and later, as already mentioned, this trio were the founding members of The Denver Showband.

Derek was not included in The Denver Showband line-up, and it was not until some years later, when he was invited to join Harry Martin, Eamonn Campbell and Twick Donnelly, as bass guitarist with The Country Gents, that his show business career really began. His successful performances with this outfit soon led to his recruitment by the Tigermen Showband, and culminated in an

Derek McCormack

Derek McCormack with The Furey Brothers.

Derek McCormack with The Barleycorn.

invitation to join Dermot O'Brien and The Clubmen.

Shortly after his exit from The Dermot O'Brien Trio, Derek was invited to join the hugely successful ballad group The Barleycorn. The group consisted of John Delaney (banjo and mandolin), Denis O'Rourke (violin), and Paddy Sweeney (acoustic guitar). Derek assumed the role of bass guitarist and vocalist, and although Paddy Sweeney had other musical interests, which very often meant that The Barleycorn performed as a three piece outfit, nevertheless, the personnel continued unaltered throughout the 1980s and into the 1990s.

The group travelled the globe, and their appearances attracted huge audiences. Their recordings, which very often featured the fantastic singing voice of Derek, sold extensively throughout the world. Their many recordings are still sought after, and in Australia in particular, this demand is quite remarkable. The decision to disband The Barleycorn was taken during a tour of Australia in the latter half of 1995. The group agreed to fulfil their immediate list of bookings, and their last gig together took place aboard The Irish Festival Cruise in January 1996.

Following the disbandment of The Barleycorn, Derek embarked on a solo career, and during this period he formed a close relationship with the chart topping Furey Brothers folk group. The Fureys invited him to join their group and, over a period of several years, he managed to combine his appearances with them, while still pursuing his own solo career. He also formed a three piece group called Nickelodeon, which comprised Derek (acoustic guitar), Ronnie Kennedy (accordion) and Billy Condon (violin). Ronnie and Billy were both members of The Daniel O'Donnell band, and just like Derek, they managed to confine their appearances with Nickelodeon to occasions which did not clash with their other commitments. Following this rather hectic time in his career, Derek decided to take things a little easier and began to concentrate much more on his solo career.

During his time with The Barleycorn, Derek was featured on numerous recordings, and included amongst these were three major hit singles entitled "My Cavan Girl", "A Song For Ireland", and "Roisin".

CHAPTER THIRTY

BORN TO BE A DRUMMER

As I have now reported on the careers of Eamonn Campbell, Harry Martin, and Derek McCormack, three members of the four piece outfit known as The Country Gents, this seems like an appropriate place to complete my account of this great group by including some details of the group's fourth member and drummer, John (Twick) Donnelly.

Twick was taught to play drums by his father Peter, who was one of the founding members of The Flying Carlton Orchestra. During the late 1950s he was invited to play drums with The Crilly School of Music Band. He accompanied this band on many of their variety show appearances, and he also made several broadcasts on Radio Eireann during his time with them. As can be seen in some of my earlier reports, he went on to play with many Drogheda based bands during the late 1950s and throughout the early 1960s. In early 1965 he decided to embark on a professional career with The Odeon Showband from Dublin. This band was an offshoot from the famous Mick Delahunty Orchestra from Clonmel. For a while, The Odeon enjoyed considerable success, but when they succeeded in recruiting top vocalist Roly Daniels, and adopted the new name of The Memphis Showband, their success stepped up a gear. They soon became a major attraction and played to capacity audiences at venues throughout the country.

Following the departure of Roly Daniels and the subsequent disbanding of the Memphis Showband, Twick joined The Country Gents. When this outfit decided to call it a day, he embarked on a succession of gigs with various outfits, before eventually teaming up with Jim Kavanagh and The New Sound in early 1972, and with whom he continued to perform for the next couple of decades.

The popularity of singing lounges and cabaret venues grew quite rapidly during the latter half of the 1960s, and this in turn led to a demand for many of the Showband musicians to provide the musical entertainment for these shows. This significant change in the public's choice of entertainment was not lost on the managers of these venues, and it wasn't long before they began to provide dance floors for the use of their ever increasing number of punters. Although I am dealing specifically with Drogheda and the surrounding area, a similar situation was also occurring in Dublin, and indeed, nationwide.

With the rise in popularity of cabaret, and the combination of Showband members becoming increasingly involved in that scene, coupled with the decision of cabaret managers to provide dancing facilities at their venues, it soon became apparent that the days of the showband phenomenon were numbered.

CHAPTER THIRTY ONE
GEORGIE'S HOTSPOT

Before I report on some of Drogheda's leading showbands of the 1960s who successfully made the transition and embraced the new culture of cabaret etc. it should be pointed out that the popularity of singing lounges and cabaret spots was not entirely an overnight sensation that occurred in the late 1960s. The seeds for this form of entertainment in Drogheda were firmly sown much earlier at a venue on Merchant's Quay in Drogheda.

For a while during the early 1960s, Georgie's Bar, also known locally as Georgie's Night Spot, laid claim to the title of Drogheda's first bar and cabaret lounge.

Initially, many local musicians provided the entertainment there, but as the venue grew in popularity, it began to attract musicians and audiences from a much wider area.

Our band rarely played on Monday nights, and during our time with The Toppers Showband, Mickey suggested that we should form a trio from part of our band and look for Monday bookings at Georgies. Although Tommy Leddy was very unhappy about this arrangement and refused to take part, we went ahead anyway.

During that time, a little known Dublin group called The Ronnie Drew Ballad Group were regularly featured at Georgies, and yes it was that same group of musicians who later changed their name to that of The Dubliners and went on to achieve international fame.

These lads accepted the proceeds of a "Cover Charge", which they collected at the door, as part payment for their appearances at Georgies. In addition, they asked Georgie to supply them with "a few drinks" as an added bonus.

I recall a conversation which took place when Mickey first approached

Georgie in pursuit of a few Monday night gigs for us. I overheard Georgie stipulate that there must be no complimentary drinks included in our payment arrangements. I thought that this request was very odd until Mickey explained how Georgie had been very unhappy with the agreement he had entered into with Ronnie and the boys.

Georgie said that he had greatly underestimated the group's capacity for drinking pints, and that the continued viability of his business was in jeopardy. Our time at Georgie's was rather short lived, and to Tommy's relief, we discontinued the arrangement. As I have already outlined, this was not to be the end of our venture into the lounge bar and cabaret circuit. A few years later, when we were playing with The Chancellors Showband, Mickey again suggested the setting up of a sub group within that band, similar to that of a few years earlier.

McNally's bar was an old and long established pub situated on Wellington Quay in Drogheda. Following a change of ownership during the mid 1960s, the new proprietor carried out an extensive renovation of the premises. The bar area was refurbished, but more significantly, a large lounge area was added to the rear of the building, and the establishment was re-named The Boyne Tavern Lounge Bar.

The new owner was acquainted with Mickey and following some discussions between the pair, we were encouraged to form a group similar to that which had performed at Georgies Lounge. The suggested group was to be made up of four members of The Chancellors Showband, and they were Mickey Rooney, (vocalist), Paddy Toner (drums), Tony Cassidy (bass guitar) and I played lead guitar.

We were offered a significant number of advance bookings, and the terms were also quite enticing. We held a meeting with the other members of the band, and as expected, Tommy Leddy again voiced his opposition to this arrangement.

However, this time around, Tommy predicted the inevitable demise of our entire band, and although it was not obvious to us at the time, a few short years later, his prediction was to prove spot on. Despite Tommy's foreboding we went ahead with the plan, and performed at The Boyne Tavern on a regular basis.

This new arrangement meant that we were playing most nights of the week, and on some occasions, we played two gigs on the same night. Having played at The Tavern gig, we then packed our gear and headed off to play somewhere else with the full band. Obviously with all of this performing, not only did we improve as a unit, the overall band performances were also enhanced.

In order to provide an adequate view of the situation prevailing at the time, I have included a copy of an article that appeared in The Drogheda Independent in June 1968, which not only deals with our appearances at The Tavern, but amply describes the public's changing tastes in entertainment during the late 1960s.

Nevertheless, we had a great time with many highlights, during the final couple of years of The Chancellors Showband. We had more bookings than we could cope with, and our gigs continued to attract very large audiences. So, before I bring the curtain down on this great period, I will conclude with a last look back at this fine band.

In my long and varied career in entertainment, I have encountered many fine singers, but in my view, Mickey Rooney, our lead vocalist was surely one of the finest performers with whom I have had the pleasure of sharing a stage. Because of my association with Mickey over the years, it might appear that my opinion may be somewhat biased, so I refer again to The Drogheda Independent article of June 1968, which quite adequately describes the wonderful voice and personality of Mickey Rooney.

The summer season dances at The Golf Club in Bettystown would certainly be right up there amongst the bands' more memorable high points. We played at these gigs on alternative weekends during the latter half of the 1960s. Birch McLoughlin and The Trolls occupied the other slots, and all of these gigs were invariably full-house affairs.

The dance hall area at Bettystown Golf Club was a converted assembly hall

Mickey and Group are tops in Lounge Entertainment

On two occasions in the past few months the name of Mickey Rooney, lead singer with the Chancellors Showband, crept up in the official weekly Pop magazine "Spotlight" and we quote a letter to the Editor of that publication:—

"Dear Editor,

I heard a singer down at Clogherhead and I'm told that he plays with some band. I think he's marvellous at 'There Goes My Everything,' 'Funny Forgotten Feeling,' 'Oh What A Night' and other great hits. He could put some of our better known showband singers to shame. Who is he and what showband does he belong to—Joan Wright, Drimnagh."

The singer referred to was, of course, Mickey Rooney.

And on another occasion in the popular "Insight" column the following appeared. "There is a singer in Drogheda called Mickey Rooney with the Chancellors Showband and he's worth listening to."

Since these references appeared Mickey, while not forsaking the Show, has branched out in a new field, that of Lounge Entertainment and in this sphere of show business he is rapidly adding to the good name that he already has.

Backed by three members of the Chancellors, Harry Reilly, Tony Cassidy and Paddy Toner he has taken over the entertainment spot at the very popular Boyne Tavern and since his first appearance, this venue has become a "must" with a very large number of patrons both from Drogheda and surrounding areas as far away as Dublin City.

That Mickey is a first class entertainer is verified by the owner of the establishment, Mr. Laughlin, who said "Mickey and the boys are really top class and I have had no end of praise for their performances here on the week-ends from a big number of our patrons."

EXTENSIVE REPERTOIRE

The repertoire of this talented group is, indeed, extensive and their playing, and the singing by Mickey, of such popular numbers as "Chance of a Lifetime," "Man Without Love," "Land of a Thousand Dances," "If I Only Had Time," "Delilah" and "Simon Says" is very well received. The latter is a show-stopper and is really the one which "brings down the house" nightly. The system in the Boyne is as in most other lounges with request cards available to the customers but Mickey Rooney, who also performs the M.C. duties, has an unique ability of being able to get his customers up on the rostrum without much ado and therefore sees to it that the show runs without a hitch from start to finish.

Lounge entertainment now looks as if it has come to stay as people nowadays seem to get as much enjoyment out of listening to their friends performing and, indeed, giving a little stave themselves, and this being so the Boyne Tavern with its very talented group under the leadership of Mickey Rooney, seems assured of a great future in this field. Those who once patronise is, always return and for those who have not been, a bit of advce—it is well worth the visit !

Mickey Rooney: Cutting from Drogheda Independent 1968.

with a make-shift stage, and the stage itself was simply a wooden platform supported by a collection of beer barrels.

We followed the same routine on every dance night, whereby we set up our gear, tuned up our instruments, and when we were ready to start proceedings, we were joined on stage by our vocalist Mickey.

One night (which we later referred to as the night Mickey brought the house down) the hall was already quite full before he made his usual entrance. He marched through the assembled crowd, and in an effort to appear really cool, he gave a little hop and skip, before leaping onto the stage. Unfortunately he caught his foot on the edge of the temporary structure, and as he crashed onto the stage, everything was sent flying. There were microphones and amplifiers everywhere. Luckily there was nothing damaged except Mickey's ego.

In 1969, when another lounge bar called The Royal House on Georges Street decided to go down the same route as The Boyne Tavern, the management invited our four piece outfit to perform at their venue as well as The Tavern. This increased activity of the sub group within The Chancellors Showband put a big strain on the continued survival of The Showband, and almost inevitably led to its disbandment.

The end for The Chancellors was a rather subdued affair, and it came in late 1969. We were probably just tired of the same old routine, and one night at a rehearsal someone suggested that perhaps it was time to disband. Most of us nodded in agreement, and the decision was taken to fulfil our remaining bookings and to call it a day. Although this meant the end for The Chancellors, our four piece outfit continued with our gigs at The Tavern and The Royal House.

Our final night was a rather sombre affair. Not only was this the end of the band, but it was most likely the end of a great era.

The end of the 1960s may have brought the curtain down on our Showband days, but the friendships we established were set to continue.

CHAPTER THIRTY TWO

THE PUB CABARET

As I have already indicated, we were by no means trailblazers, merely part of a trend, and many other showbands took the same route as ourselves. When The Denver Showband disbanded in late 1967, four of their members took the decision to form a new outfit they called The Keymen. The group consisted of Roy McCormack (lead guitar), Terry Heeney (bass guitar), John (Twick) Donnelly (drums), and Brendan Crean (vocals).

They succeeded in securing regular bookings at The Boyne Tavern, and they alternated their appearances with our outfit at this venue. In addition to The Tavern gigs, they played at numerous weddings and reunions. In 1968, they secured a summer season of gigs in The Staff Bar at Butlins Holiday Camp. When Brendan Crean decided to exit the group, he was replaced by Sean Reynolds on guitar and vocals. The Keymen decided to call it a day in early 1969, and following their disbandment, all of these talented musicians secured positions with various other outfits, and their names are set to reappear.

Meanwhile, also during that same year, our four piece outfit was appearing less frequently at The Boyne Tavern and was accepting considerably more bookings at The Royal House, when Tony Cassidy decided to take a lengthy break from the music scene. Roy McCormack was the obvious choice to replace Tony, as he had been a regular substitute for our group during absences by both Tony and me, and was now available due to the disbandment of The Keymen.

In early 1970, I also decided to take a break from music, and my temporary retirement led to a reshuffle within the group. Roy assumed the role of lead guitarist, and Kenny Doyle became the new fourth member when he augmented the group on keyboards. This four piece group remained unchanged

The New Sound:
Kenny Doyle, John (Twick) Donnelly, Jim Kavanagh, Roy McCormack.

The Underworld:
Murragh O'Brien, Bob McGuffin, Val Rogers,
Francie McLoughlin, Dessie (Edger) Gray, Tom McCann.

throughout the remainder of that year, and the line-up consisted of Mickey Rooney (vocals), Roy McCormack (lead guitar), Kenny Doyle (keyboards) and Paddy Toner (drums).

When Mickey Rooney exited the group in early 1971, he was replaced by Jim Kavanagh, and the group assumed the name of The New Sound. There was just one more change in The New Sound's personnel, and this occurred in 1972 when Paddy Toner took the decision to retire from music. He was replaced by John (Twick) Donnelly on drums, and this line-up remained intact for the entire lifetime of the group.

Jim Kavanagh and The New Sound continued to perform for the next two decades, and were widely acclaimed as being one of the finest groups to emerge from the Showband era. Indeed, as well as being one of our finest groups, they also went on to become one of the longest surviving groups on the local scene.

In the late 1980s, Jim Kavanagh and Kenny Doyle formed a two piece outfit known as Jim and Kenny, and they continued to perform as a duo whilst maintaining their commitment to The New Sound. On the disbandment of The New Sound in the early 1990s, Jim and Kenny decided to carry on as a two piece, but in 1993, they also took the decision to disband.

In the early 1970s I was approached by Derek Fagan's father to give some guitar lessons to his son, and I agreed. Derek very quickly became quite proficient, and in 1993, after several years performing with a number of groups, he teamed up with Jim Kavanagh. They formed a two piece outfit known as Jim and Derek, and they continued to perform until 2005, when Jim took the decision to finally call it a day. Derek continues to perform right up to the present day.

Prior to his involvement with The New Sound, Jim Kavanagh had been performing as lead singer with a couple of leading outfits of the 1960s. His first group was known as The Underworld. This outfit had evolved from a Showband which had been performing under the name of The Checkmates. However, the group had no connection with the previously mentioned showband of the same name. As the original version of The Checkmates had already been

The City Showband: Jim Kavanagh, Bob McGuffin, Tom McCann, Eddie Barrett, Murrough O'Brien, Francie McLoughlin, Raphael Kierans.

disbanded, and the members had all moved on, this most recent outfit had merely decided to adopt the title.

This latest version of The Checkmates Showband was assembled and managed by Terry Skelly, who, as already mentioned, had earlier been one of the founding members of The Flying Aces Dance Band. The line-up consisted of Val Rogers (lead guitar), Francie McLoughlin (rhythm guitar), Tom McCann (bass guitar), Raymie White (drums), Gerry Connor (trombone), Dessie (Skinner) Fay (saxophone and guitar), and Bob McGuffin (keyboards). The band enjoyed quite a deal of success during the remainder of 1966, but at the beginning of 1967 they took the decision to dispense with their management and their showband image, and to regroup under the banner of The Underworld.

Four of the former Showband members who were included in the original line-up for The Underworld were Val Rogers, Francie McLoughlin, Tom McCann, and Bob McGuffin. They were joined by Murrough O'Brien (drums), and Dessie (Edger) Gray, (lead vocalist). This six piece outfit enjoyed a very successful career, and built up a significant fan base during the latter half of the 1960s. They appeared regularly at such venues as The Television Club in Dublin's Harcourt Street and The Palm Beach in Portmarnock Dublin, but they were probably best remembered for their regular spots in Drogheda's Abbey Ballroom. They were also the regular support group for The Jim Farrelly Big Band, and Jim hired them for most of his gigs along Ireland's east coast.

There were just two personnel changes in the Underworld's original line-up, and these occurred during 1968. When Dessie (Edger) Gray exited the group, he was replaced by lead vocalist Jim Kavanagh, and shortly afterwards, when Val Rogers decided to follow suit, he was replaced by Hugh McCormack on lead guitar. Incidentally, when keyboards player Bob McGuffin took a few weeks break from the group to pursue his studies, his replacement was none other than country singing star Gloria. Gloria, of course, went on to score a massive hit with her recording of "One Day At A Time".

The Abbey Ballroom represented a very large proportion of The

Underworld's engagements, and the ballroom's demise in February 1969, dealt a huge blow to the morale of the group, ultimately leading to their decision to disband shortly afterwards.

Hugh McCormack decided to embark on a career as a professional musician, and played with a succession of top professional outfits such as Pat McGeegan and The Skyrockets, Gene and The Lions, and The Graduates Showband. In the early 1970s he returned to college to continue his studies, and having subsequently qualified as an accountant, he now heads up his own accountancy business. However, throughout his college days, he continued with his musical career, and played guitar with other professional outfits such as Gary Street and The Fairways, singing star Sandy Kelly (Duskey), and finally, The Jack Ruane Showband. Hughie continues with his musical career on a part time basis, and is currently a member of The Two Tone Blues band, which also features his old pal Tom McCann on bass guitar. Hughie is also a keen collector of guitars and possesses a large collection of both vintage and modern instruments.

Meanwhile the remaining five members of The Underworld decided to try their hand at forming another showband. To this end they recruited two new musicians, Eddie Barrett (trumpet) and Raphael Kierans (trumpet). The new outfit became known as The City Showband, and Joe Dunne acted as their manager.

The line-up of The City Showband consisted of Jim Kavanagh (lead vocalist), Francie McLoughlin (lead guitar), Tom McCann (bass guitar), Bob McGuffin (keyboards), Murrough O'Brien (drums), together with trumpeters Eddie Barrett and Raphael Kierans. Unfortunately, as the public's enthusiasm for showbands in general was already on the wane, this venture turned out to be a rather short lived affair and they disbanded before the end of 1969.

Although this was to be the end of yet another Showband, as with so many other outfits, the demise of The City Showband led to the creation of several other smaller outfits, and I will include them in the concluding section of the book.

* * * * * * * * * *

In 1965, when Louis Smith took the decision to disband The Delta Boys Showband, most of the musicians who made up the fifth and final version of that band dispersed and secured positions with various other outfits. However, the band's lead singer Michael (Mickey) Black decided to take an extended break from the music scene.

Prior to his time with The Delta Boys, Mickey had long been regarded as one of the town's leading vocalists. In the late 1950s he teamed up with John Moore and Jim Finglas and together they formed a three piece vocal group known as The Prefects. The three guys adopted this name because all three had previously acted as prefects at The Boys Club in Yellowbatter. Initially, The Boys Club became the cornerstone of their earliest gigs, but it wasn't long before they were a regular feature on most other local variety shows. Sometime

The Sonna Boys:
Pa Carter, Bruce Moran, Mickey Black, Larry Carolan.

The Sonna Boys:
Bruce Moran, Mickey Black, Larry Carolan, Pa Carter.

The Prefects:
John Moore, Jim Finglas, Mickey Black.

after their formation The Prefects became a four piece outfit when they were joined by guitarist/singer Pat (Pa) Carter. As the group was basically a variety act, this allowed each of the members to pursue other musical interests, whilst continuing to perform as The Prefects. This loose arrangement ensured the survival and continued success of the group for many more years.

In the early 1960s, Mickey's first opportunity to sing with a dance band came about, when he was invited by Fintan Stanley to join his group for a series of gigs at The Laurel Park Ballroom near Bray, Co Wicklow. The Ray Allen Orchestra was the anchor group at Laurel Park, and Fintan's group, as the featured guest act, was required to give two separate performances nightly. The group's line-up consisted of Fintan, (accordion), Mickey (vocals), Jimmy Fitzpatrick (bass), Mick Alexander (saxophone/clarinet), and Tommy (Bongo) Donnelly (drums). Following the completion of these series of gigs, and the subsequent dissolution of The Delta Boys, as already mentioned, Mickey took an extended break from the music scene.

The end of the 1960s and the beginning of the 1970s was, in general, a time of significant change in the public's taste in entertainment. The progression of The New Sound, and how they dealt with the decline of the dance hall culture, through to the emergence and subsequent rise of the lounge-bar and cabaret culture, is a fairly typical example of how most other bands dealt with the situation, and they adapted themselves accordingly.

The changing entertainment scene of the late 1960s did not escape the attention of local businessman Jim Kierans, who was at that time the proprietor of a hairdressing salon on Stockwell Street in Drogheda. He took the decision to get involved in the music business by applying his managerial skills to the handling and promotion of bands/groups and musicians, who found themselves in this new evolving situation. To this end he opened an office on West Street where he set up The Jay Kay Promotions Agency. He established a network of venues in which his clients could perform and very soon afterwards he had numerous acts on his books.

At Jim's suggestion, Mickey Black came out of retirement, and together with

Tracks:
Dessie (Skinner) Fay, Paddy (PC) Caffrey, Ben Corcoran, Brendan McConnon,
Tony McCormack, Dave Donnelly, Carl Phillips (Centre)

Larry Carolan (keyboards), Pa Carter (guitar), and Bruce Moran (drums), they formed the group known as The Sonna Boys. Jim Kierans took over as manager and very soon they were playing at a variety of venues. Also under Jim's management, the group secured a series of weekly gigs as the resident group at The Village Hotel in Bettystown. In 1969, The Sonna Boys made a successful TV appearance on The Ulster Television show Teatime With Tommy.

However, from the outset, Jim had decided to concentrate on the public's growing interest in the cabaret scene, and his main aim was to provide acts for the ever increasing number of venues providing floor shows. One of his earliest successes came when he secured a contract to provide the entertainment for a series of weekly floor shows at The Boyne Valley Hotel in Drogheda and, as many of the featured acts for these shows required the services of a resident backing group, Jim, of course, secured that position for his protégés, The Sonna Boys.

However, when Larry Carolan decided to exit the group to join up with John Leonard and his group at The Drake Inn, Finglas, The Sonna Boys underwent a major revamp. Jim Kierans recruited the internationally renowned musician Paddy Neary (accordion/piano), Nicky Callan (trumpet and guitar) and in addition, he persuaded me to end my short break from music and to return to the stage of The Boyne Valley Hotel as lead guitarist with this new version of his group. Although Mickey Black continued to perform with the group, he gradually assumed the more prominent role of cabaret artiste, and for the duration of our term at The Boyne Valley Hotel, the group became known as Paddy Neary and The Sonna Boys. At the end of a very successful cabaret series this particular version of the group dispersed

Jim once again revamped the group and, with Mickey Black as lead vocalist, The Sonna Boys continued to perform for a few more years appearing at many local venues and at various weddings and reunions. Included amongst the numerous other musicians who performed under the banner of The Sonna Boys were Martin Quinn, Harry Martin, Ramie Smith, Paddy Byrne, and Liam (Smiley) Reilly.

Following the dissolution of The Sonna Boys all of the group's members secured positions with various other outfits, and although both Mickey Black and Martin Quinn also lined up with separate outfits, they formed an enduring partnership as a two piece outfit. They performed under the name of M. & M. and the partnership remained intact for decades. In 1990, when they were booked for a summer season at The Match Maker Bar in Lisdoonvarna, they were so popular that they were re-booked for several more summer season gigs.

Several years after the dissolution of The Sonna Boys, Pa Carter teamed up with a group of local musicians and having secured a series of regular gigs at the recreation centre of The O'Raghallaigh's Gaelic Football Club, they soon built up a significant following. With tongues firmly in cheek, they chose the name of "Rubbish" for their five piece outfit, and with a line-up which featured Tom Sinnott on vocals together with Gene Brady (lead guitar), Pa Carter (rhythm guitar) Joe McLouglin (keyboards), and Ben Moonan (drums), they enjoyed a great innings, and they certainly belied their chosen name.

****

Guitarist Ben Corcoran, another local musician with a long and illustrious musical career, also spent some time during the early 1970s under the management of Jim Kierans and Jay Kay Promotions. Ben bought his first guitar for just £3 in Waltons music shop in Dublin during the early 1960s. Like so many other guitarists, including myself, he also purchased a copy of Bert Weedon's "Play In A Day" guitar tuition book, together with a collection of records by The Shadows.

Ben made his guitar playing debut during an early 1960s gig at The Golf Club in Bettystown, when he was invited on stage by his friend and neighbour Phil McLoughlin, to play guitar with Phil's group The Road Runners. Later that year, on a summer school term visit to An Gaeltacht, Ranafast, Co. Donegal, both Ben and Phil decided to enter a talent contest being held there. To boost their chances of success, they enlisted the services of another guitarist to accompany them on stage, and the trio went on to win the competition outright. Ben told me that he began referring in jest to their guest guitarist as "the little red headed fellow", and even though this third member of the prize winning trio is better known today as the international singing star Paul Brady, Ben and Paul have remained firm friends ever since, and Ben still affectionately uses this term whenever they meet up.

In 1964, when Eamonn Campbell was preparing for his leaving cert exams, he opted for a three month break from playing music with Louis Smith's Delta Boys, and at Eamonn's suggestion, Ben was chosen to act as substitute guitarist for the duration. Not only was Ben delighted to get his first opportunity to play with an established showband, he also got to use Eamonn's top of the range guitar amplification. Over the next few years, Ben took a break from the music scene to continue with his studies. He also used this period to devote what spare time he had to improving his guitar playing skills.

In the late 1960s, having spent some time rehearsing together, Ben and a few of his musician friends, took the decision to try their hand at forming a Showband. To this end they set about including a brass section in their line-up. The new outfit was called Dawn and the line-up included Ben (guitar), P.C. Caffrey (drums), Dave Donnelly (keyboards), Dessie (Skinner) Fay (tenor sax), and Tony McCormack (tenor sax). With local record shop owner Kevin Breen taking over the management of the group, their popularity soon began to soar. They travelled extensively throughout Ireland and they also toured England where they played in selected Irish clubs. Back home, they secured regular bookings at Drogheda's Palm Court Ballroom where they played support band to many top international acts, such as The Tremelos, The Move, and The Equals. The group continued with their successful run, until Easter 1971, when the decision was taken to bring the curtain down on Dawn and to re-group under a new name and with a new manager.

During the band's successful run, there were several other musicians who also played with Dawn and they included Mo Conlon (bass), Frankie Smith (trumpet), Declan Thompson (vocals), and Pat Fitzpatrick (bass).

The dissolution of Dawn in 1971 was followed almost immediately by the formation of a new outfit. When Jim Kierans succeeded in persuading most of the outfit's former members to re-group under his management, he also persuaded them to adopt the new name of Tracks. At that time, Jim was manager to cabaret star Carl Phillips, and his intention was to have a group who were prepared to give priority to any bookings for which Carl required support. The line-up for this new group included Ben Corcoran (guitar), P.C. Caffrey (drums), Dessie (Skinner) Fay (tenor sax), Dave Donnelly (keyboards), Tony McCormack (tenor sax), and Brendan McConnon, (trombone). Tracks took up where Dawn left off, and throughout the remainder of 1971, and for part of 1972, their successful run continued. With Carl Phillips acting, on occasions, as front man for the group, they were without doubt a top class cabaret act and the group were featured at many of Ireland's major cabaret venues. The decision to bring the curtain down on Tracks was taken during 1972, and the musicians went their separate ways.

****

Sometime afterwards during the 1970s, Ben Corcoran teamed up with Paddy Kelly in the hugely successful full-time outfit known as Reunion. I have included a report on both musicians and their group Reunion in the final section of this book. However, prior to his involvement with Reunion, Paddy Kelly had spent some time as the featured singer with another outfit known as The Diamonds, and this seems like a suitable place to include my report on

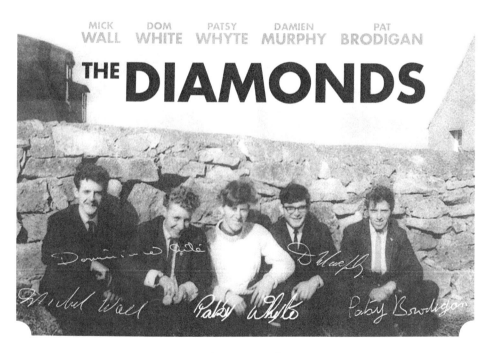

The Diamonds:
Mickey Wall, Dom White, Patsy White, Damien Murphy, Patsy Brodigan.

that outfit.

During the summer of 1964, a new four piece outfit emerged under the banner of The Diamonds. The original line-up consisted of Aidan Gough (lead guitar), P.J. Mooney (bass guitar), John Joe Cooper (saxophone), and Dodo Carey (drums). Some months afterwards when Dodo decided to exit the group, Patsy White was chosen as his replacement on drums. However, prior to his enrolment with The Diamonds, Patsy suggested that they should consider going forward as a five piece outfit, and having convinced the other three members of the merits of his suggestion, he further persuaded them that this new fifth member should be his brother Dominic (Dom) White (rhythm guitar).

The new five piece line-up consisting of Aidan Gough, P.J. Mooney, John Joe Cooper, Patsy White, and Dom White, began an intensive period of rehearsals in The I.C.A. hall on Donore Road Drogheda, and if this particular venue sounds familiar, well yes it is also the same venue, The Hut, where The Chancellors Showband conducted their rehearsals, and the caretaker was indeed the mother of Patsy and Dom.

The Diamonds secured their first gig in The Parochial Hall, Donore village, and following a successful debut performance, they were booked to appear at Drogheda's Abbey Ballroom as the support act for one of Ireland's leading outfits of the 1960s, The Dixies Showband. Although they felt intimidated about playing before such a huge audience, they acquitted themselves quite well, and following the evening's entertainment, they received an offer from The Dixie's manager which would have them appear at all of his band's gigs along the entire east coast of Ireland. They eagerly accepted his offer and the career of The Diamonds was well and truly launched. The arrangement with The Dixies did not prevent them from performing at other gigs, and they were much in demand to perform at various parochial halls and reunions etc., throughout the region.

Their successful run continued uninterrupted for the next four years, and for a few weeks during the summer of each of those years, they got to enjoy a taste of being full-time professionals. They turned their annual holidays from their regular employment into that of a busman's holiday by travelling throughout the entire country performing with The Dixies. The group's manager and regular driver was a Mrs Gough from Slane village. She not only took care of their booking arrangements and their safe passage to and from gigs, but she also looked after the welfare of her young protégés.

The Diamonds underwent a major change in personnel at the end of the 1960s with the departure of three of its original members and the recruitment of three replacement musicians. The new look Diamonds that emerged and continued performing during the next three years consisted of Dom White (lead guitar), Mickey Wall (rhythm guitar), Damian Murphy (bass guitar), Patsy White (drums), and Patsy Brodigan (vocals).

When Patsy Brodigan took the decision to exit the group, he was replaced by Paddy Kelly on vocals. Paddy was already recognised locally as a future singing star, and his appearances with The Diamonds during their gigs with The Dixies, quickly gained him national recognition. Despite receiving numerous tempting offers from other groups, Paddy remained with The Diamonds for the next eighteen months before finally accepting an offer to join the group known as Reunion.

Following the departure of Paddy Kelly, the decision was taken to continue as a four piece outfit, and the line-up of Dom White, Mickey Wall, Damian Murphy, and Patsy White continued to represent The Diamonds during the remainder of that group's prolonged and successful innings. The curtain finally fell on one of Drogheda's longest surviving outfits in 1998.

CHAPTER THIRTY THREE

CHANGES, NEW BEGINNINGS & EVEN A STINT IN CANADA

In 1969, Alan Barton (drums), together with his two friends Paul McGee (lead guitar), and Jim Coyle (bass guitar), had been rehearsing in each other's homes for some time before they took the decision to try their hand at performing in public. As a means of launching their new group, they decided to enter a talent contest in The Royal House Lounge Bar in Drogheda, where they performed under the name of Revolution. They not only won their heat of the competition, but also won through to the grand final and the publicity they received resulted in the group receiving a substantial number of local gigs. During the latter half of 1970, they received a major boost when they were chosen to act as the regular support outfit for Dermot O'Brien and The Clubmen. This arrangement led to Revolution being booked to perform at most of The Clubmen's gigs within a 60 mile radius of Drogheda.

In 1971, when Jim Coyle exited the group, both Alan Barton and Paul McGee decided to stay together and to form a new group. With the recruitment of David Kelly (rhythm guitar), John Kelly (bass guitar) and Johnny Monaghan (vocalist), this new five piece outfit became known as Redwood. The line-up continued unaltered for the next few years and during that time, Redwood established themselves as one of the most popular outfits on the local circuit. In 1974, when David and John Kelly decided to move on, the three remaining members of the group set about recruiting two new musicians, and to continue as before, with a five piece outfit under the banner of Redwood. The new look outfit consisted of Paul McGee (lead guitar), Tom Reilly (bass guitar), Don Chesser (keyboards), Alan Barton (drums) and Johnny Monaghan (vocals).

In 1975, when Alan Barton took the decision to move on, he was replaced on drums by Gerry Fahy, and Redwood continued with their successful career. Meanwhile Alan embarked on a long and distinguished career in entertainment, and when John Leonard assumed the role of singer and M.C. at the Drake Inn Cabaret Lounge in Finglas Dublin, Alan was recruited to fill the vacant position of drummer with The Drake's resident backing group. He remained in this role until 1976, when he was invited to join the Brannigan Brothers. Although their sister Geraldine was no longer a member of the group, The Brannigans remained a major attraction throughout the country. In 1977 Alan joined a North Dublin based outfit known as Stage 2, and later that year he played with local group Daylight Robbery.

In 1978 he was invited to re-join his old band mates from Redwood who had re-formed under the new name of Nitebus. The line-up consisted of Alan (drums), Paul McGee (lead guitar), Tom Reilly (bass guitar) and Johnny Monaghan (vocals).

In 1979 he was invited to join country singer star Margot and her band, remaining with this outfit for two years. In 1981 he continued his full time professional career, when he joined The Cotton Mill Boys. He remained with this outfit until 1986, and later that same year Alan teamed up with another top outfit when he accepted an invitation from Spyder Simpson to join his band.

In 1988, country singing star Mary Duff invited him to join her band and he spent the next four years with this outfit. In 1993 when B.B. Berrill decided to exit top local outfit Custers Last Band, Alan was chosen as his replacement. He remained with this group until 2004, and the line-up consisted of Mick Doherty (lead guitar), Gerry Mulroy (rhythm guitar), Paul Martin (bass guitar), Phil O'Neill (steel guitar), and Alan Barton (drums).

Finally, Alan once again teamed up with some of his old band mates from Redwood in a new group they named Smooch. The line-up for this outfit consists of Paul McGee (lead guitar), Colin O'Dowd, (rhythm guitar), Tom Reilly (bass guitar), and Alan (drums).

****

The Square Penny was yet another outfit to emerge during the late 1960s, and like so many other groups of that era, their career can also be traced back to a combination of school pals holding rehearsals in each others homes. The original line-up consisted of Tommy Victory (lead guitar), Oliver Tinsley (rhythm guitar), and Mickey Munster (drums). Some time afterwards, when Oliver Tinsley exited the group, and with the recruitment of both Tom Reilly (bass guitar), and Paddy Reilly (vocals), they became a four piece outfit.

The group made their debut appearance in The Community Hall in Julianstown Co Meath, and at the end of this gig, they were approached by local man Bobby Russell who offered to become their manager. They accepted Bobby's offer, and this decision proved to be the making of The Square Penny. Bobby quickly set about getting some bookings into his diary, and the group built up their repertoire with a series of rehearsals in the garage adjoining Bobby's house in Julianstown.

Not long afterwards, they were playing in such venues as The Palm Court and The Abbey Ballroom in Drogheda. They were also regularly booked for The Ashling Ballroom Clogherhead, and The T.V. Club in Harcourt Street, Dublin. During the next few years, there were two further changes to the group's line-up. Paddy Reilly decided to exit the group and Tom Reilly accepted an offer to team up with The Trolls. In the aftermath of these changes, and with the recruitment of Maurice Victory on bass guitar and Stephen McCann on keyboards, the group continued as a four piece outfit.

1972 was a career changing year for The Square Penny. When they and numerous other groups auditioned for the opportunity to play a series of gigs on a six month tour of Newfoundland and the east coast of Canada, The Pennies emerged victorious. Prior to this momentous tour, the group took the decision to become a five piece outfit, and to this end they recruited Liz King as their new vocalist. The line-up for The Canadian tour consisted of Tommy Victory (lead guitar), Maurice Victory (bass guitar), Stephen McCann (keyboards), Mickey Munster (drums), and Liz King (vocalist).

The Square Penny:
Pat Finnegan (Roadie), Maurice Victory, Tom Victory, Mickey Munster.

SQUARE
PENNY

The Square Penny:
Liz King, Maurice Victory, Tom Victory, Stephen McCann, Mickey Munster.

For the duration of the tour, the group were based at St. Johns in Newfoundland, and at the suggestion of the promoters, The Square Penny were required to change their name to that of The Music Men. At the conclusion of their six month tour the group returned to Ireland.

The following year they took the decision to return to Canada and to take up where they left off, but this time around they made the journey without the comfort of a pre-arranged contract. However, they felt confident that the significant number of contacts which they had already established would see them through, and with just three of the five piece group remaining, Tommy Victory, Maurice Victory, and Mickey Munster, accompanied by Bobby Russell their manager and Pat Finnegan their road manager, and having reverted to their original name, The Square Penny set off for Canada yet again in early 1973.

This second tour proved so successful that, having built up a huge fan base and with a full diary of advance bookings, they decided that Canada was the place for them. On their return to Ireland, they immediately set about putting their affairs in order. They applied to the Canadian authorities for visas in preparation for a permanent stay there, and with the necessary paperwork under their belts, and having said their final farewells, they set off on their third and final trip to Canada.

They were greeted on arrival by promoters and fans alike, and their new career as full time entertainers took off almost immediately. They travelled extensively throughout Newfoundland, Nova Scotia, Prince Edward Island, Labrador, and New Brunswick, and their appearances invariably attracted capacity audiences. They even did a three week gig at a U. S. Base in Greenland. Following a long and successful career in Canada and whilst still at the top of their game, the decision was taken in 1982 to take things easy and to bring the curtain down on The Square Penny.

****

Redwood:
Top to bottom: Paul McGee, Don Chesser, Tom Reilly,
Johnny Monaghan, Alan Barton.

In 1969, guitarist Pat Moonan together with keyboard player Martin Weldon decided to form a new four piece outfit known as The Marksmen, and to this end they recruited fellow musicians Paddy Brady (rhythm guitar) and Ramie Smith (drums).

The success of this group was assured when, very early in their career, they secured a semi residency at The Grove Hotel, Dunleer, Co. Louth, where they were booked to perform on most Sunday nights. Not long afterwards, they became the band of choice for the management at The Neptune Hotel Bettystown, Co Meath, where they performed at many of the hotel's weddings and reunions. They quickly followed up with a further semi residency booking at Clontarf Castle in Dublin, where they were booked to perform on a monthly

The Marksmen:
Pat Moonan, Jim Reynolds, Paddy Flanagan, Martin Weldon, Eugene Kierans.

basis. The group remained intact until 1971, when Ramie Smith decided to move on and he was replaced on drums by Martin Morgan.

During 1973 when guitarist Paddy Brady accepted an offer to join another local outfit known as The Blue Beats, The Marksmen decided to re-form and to proceed as a five piece outfit. The new line-up consisted of Pat Moonan (lead guitar), Martin Weldon (keyboards), Paddy Flanagan (rhythm guitar), Martin Morgan (drums), and Jim Reynolds (vocalist).

There was just one further change in personnel. In 1974, when Martin Morgan decided to exit the group, he was replaced by Eugene (Oodie) Kierans on drums, and this final version of The Marksmen enjoyed a successful career until 1979, when the decision to disband was taken. When the group dispersed and went their separate ways, Pat Moonan in particular continued to perform with several other successful groups. I have included the details of these outfits in the final part of the book.

CHAPTER THIRTY FOUR

LOUIS THE MAESTRO, AND THE BIG BANDS

Although the remainder of this book deals primarily with the careers of many of these musicians post-1970, and the outfits with which they subsequently became associated, there is of course another part to this story, and it concerns the careers of those bands and musicians who not only survived through this period, but continued to perform and prosper for many more years. Despite the demise of many of the former dance venues, there were still quite a few that remained in operation throughout the 1970s and beyond, and they continued to attract quite sizable audiences,

Not least among these bands was the renowned Louis Smith Big Band, and it is with my account of the great man and his equally great orchestra, that I will commence the final part of this book.

A feature of the 1940s/1960s era was the Catholic Church's strong opposition to dancing during The Holy Season of Lent. As the Catholic clergy controlled most of the dance venues nationwide, the entire industry virtually came to a standstill for several weeks annually during this period.

There was not, however, the same opposition to variety shows and other such activities, and many musicians devoted much of their spare time to taking part in these events. In order to keep his band fully rehearsed and ready for the new season, Louis Smith decided to form what was to become known as The Louis Smith Big Band.

Initially, this was just meant to be a part-time venture, and remained as such for a few years before temporarily fading away. Their revival came about when Louis was asked to provide an orchestra for the Drogheda Pantomime Society

The Louis Smith Big Band:
Back: Charlie McEnteggart, Mickey Traynor, Willie Healy, Syd Kierans, Raphael Kierans, Danny Kierans, Tony Flood.
Front: Louis Smith, Martin Quinn, Valerie Kelly, Brendan Crean, Ben Mullen, Ray Buckley, Terry Smith, Sean Byrne, Kevin O'Brien.

during the late 1960s. He brought together most of the original members and also recruited several newcomers for the venture. This was to become a more permanent arrangement as the band grew in popularity and achieved tremendous success throughout the following decades. Included among their many career highlights was a performance on R.T.E's Late Late Show during the early 1990s, for which the band made their appearance under the banner of The Glen Miller Legacy.

The name change came about with the booking of Louis' big band for a performance at a major event in Cork City in late 1984. The organiser of the event decided that, as Louis's band featured quite a number of Glen Miller tunes in their repertoire, he would advertise the band as The Glen Miller Legacy. At first, Louis was not entirely happy about the use of this name, and he intended to revert to his own name following the event. However, shortly afterwards, when he realised that he quite liked the sound of the new name he decided to adopt it on a permanent basis.

The sheer number of musicians who were invited to be part of the various combinations which Louis put together to perform under the banner of his Big Bands makes it impractical to name all of them here, so in order to compensate I have included a selection of photographs bearing the various musicians' names, which I hope is fairly representative of the personnel who graced many a stage with Louis over several decades. However, what these photographs also show is that a certain male vocalist was regularly featured in both The Louis Smith big Band and The Glen Miller Legacy, and it seems appropriate that I should include here, a brief account of the career of renowned vocalist Brendan Crean.

Although it was merely coincidence that Brendan was featured amongst the cast of the 1960s pantomime which led to the re-forming of Louis' Big Band, nevertheless Louis must have been impressed by Brendan's performance, because some time afterwards he invited Brendan to become a member of his Big Band. Indeed, not only was he regularly called on to perform with Louis' Big Band over the following decades, but he was the featured vocalist with The

The Glenn Miller Legacy:
Gerry Carroll, Louis Smith, Dougie Stewart, Christy Smith, Willie Healy, Frankie Smith, Tony Flood, Johnny Milne, Brendan Crean, Kevin O'Brien, Jimmy Clynch, Ben Mullen, Terry Smith, Sean Byrne

Glen Miller Legacy for their appearance on The Late Late T.V. Show.

Brendan made his first stage appearance during the early 1960s, when he performed as guest singer with the resident group at Georgie's on Merchants Quay. As previously mentioned, over the next few years he performed as lead vocalist with several local outfits such as The Viceroys Showband and The Denver Showband, and in late 1967, he sang with The Keymen at The Boyne Tavern. Following his departure from this outfit, he was recruited as front man for The George Reilly Quintet which was the resident support act for The Jim Farrelly Big Band show at The Top Hat Ballroom in Dunlaoire. This engagement lasted for about six months and was followed by a series of summer season shows at Butlins Holiday camp.

As well as being a member of Louis' various Big Bands, both Brendan and Louis formed a successful duo and they organised these appearances to run in tandem with their other commitments. Most recently Brendan has been making a number of solo appearances with his version of The Great American Songbook and without doubt, he is still singing as well as ever.

The Glenn Miller Legacy: Back: Gerry Carroll, Frankie Smith, Freddie Reynolds (drums), Willie Healy, Nicky Callan, Bernie Bingham, Sean Cahill, Front: Louis Smith, Brendan Crean, Aidan Kavanagh, Jimmy Clynch, Mark Wilde, Donal Wynne, Matt Roberts.

CHAPTER THIRTY FIVE

BOSTON
FOR THE LONG HAUL

he Boston Showband was formed during the mid-1960s, and despite the break-up of many other showbands at the turn of that decade, they were one of the outfits which remained relatively unaffected. They continued with their showband format right through to the early years of the 1970s, so this seems like an appropriate place to include an account of yet another of our leading showbands.

The founding members of The Boston consisted of John Brannigan, Tony

The Boston Showband:
Mattie McGoona, John Woods, Tony Martin, Joe Smith, Jimmy Grey,
John Brannigan, Paddy Brannigan

The Boston Showband:
Johnny Milne, Des Smith, Tony Martin, Joe Smith, Joan Beggy, Jimmy Grey,
John Brannigan, Paddy Brannigan.

Martin, John Woods, and Jimmy Grey. As two of the original members, John Brannigan and Tony Martin hailed from Drogheda, and both John Woods and Jimmy Grey were from the Stackallen area of Co Meath, it was originally decided that the band should be known as The Boston Showband, Navan and Drogheda. Prior to the formation of The Boston, both John Brannigan and Tony Martin were already established on the local circuit having performed with several of the outfits previously mentioned in this book including The Broadway, The Flying Aces, The Viceroys, and The Adelphi.

Following the recruitment of three additional members, The Boston Showband's original seven piece line-up consisted of John Woods (vocalist), Paddy Brannigan (lead guitar), John Brannigan (rhythm guitar), Jimmy Grey (bass guitar), Mattie McGoona, (trumpet), Tony Martin (sax/clarinet) and Joe Smith (drums).

The band's first manager was Dermot Kerley, but sometime afterwards he was replaced by Ben Gordon, who was at that time manager of The

The Boston Showband:
Tony Martin, Owen Lynch, Paddy Brannigan, John Brannigan, Joe Smith

Abbey Ballroom. This arrangement led to a succession of gigs as the resident support band at The Abbey Ballroom, and also proved to be a great launch pad for the band. Not only did they get to play support for many of the top international stars who performed at The Abbey, they gained great experience from performing before capacity audiences on a nightly basis. The Boston Showband soon established themselves as a leading outfit and under Ben's management they were in demand to perform at venues nationwide.

During the latter half of the 1960s, following the departure of John Woods and Mattic McGoona, there was a significant change in personnel. The five remaining members of the band took the decision to proceed as an eight piece outfit, and to this end they recruited three new members. The new-look Boston Showband consisted of Paddy Brannigan (lead guitar), John Brannigan (rhythm guitar), Jimmy Grey (bass guitar), Des Smith (trumpet), Tony Martin (sax/clarinet), Johnny Milne (trombone), Joe Smith (drums), and Joan Beggy (vocalist). The new eight piece line-up featuring Joan Beggy

The Boston Showband, Navan

The Boston Showband:
Paddy Brannigan, Tony Martin, Mattie McGoona, Jimmy Grey, Joe Smith,
Bud McGoona, John Brannigan.

on vocals proved to be an instant hit, and the band continued with their successful run right through to the early 1970s. Although they performed at venues throughout the country, they continued to attract significant local audiences to their regular Saturday night spot at The Boyne Valley Hotel. In addition, they also performed on a regular basis at Co. Meath's Bellinter Rugby Club, and at Drogheda's Star and Crescent Club.

There was just one more major change in personnel during the lifetime of The Boston. In the aftermath of the departure of four of its members during the early part of the 1970s, the remaining four members took the decision to retain the group's name and to proceed as a five piece outfit. They recruited well known vocalist/bass guitarist Owen Lynch, and the five piece line-up of The Boston, consisting of Paddy Brannigan, John Brannigan, Tony Martin, Joe Smith, and Owen Lynch continued to entertain audiences everywhere over the course of the next couple of decades. Finally, due to the lengthy innings of The Boston, from time to time and for various reasons, several other musicians occasionally shared a stage with them. However, Pal McDonnell, well known vocalist/bass guitarist, deserves a special mention in this respect.

The Lads:
Birch McLoughlin, Shaun Black, Brian Leahy, Timmy Regan

Again:
Birch McLoughlin, Mick McLoughlin (Drums) Paul Martin, Rickki Martin.

CHAPTER THIRTY SIX

NEW CHANGES FOR THE TROLLS

In 1972, The Trolls decided to introduce a lead singer to their line-up and so they recruited vocalist Mick Doherty. The new five piece outfit had a very successful run until 1974, but following Niall Corrigan's decision to emigrate to the United States, the four remaining members decided to bring down the curtain on The Trolls.

The demise of The Trolls was soon followed by the formation of another group called The Lads. Two of the former members of The Trolls, Phil McLoughlin and Shaun Black, were joined by Timmy Regan and Brian Leahy to complete the four piece line-up.

Timmy, as I have already reported, had been a recording artiste and full time professional musician during his time as lead singer with bands such as Dermot O'Brien and The Clubmen, and The Tigermen Showband. Brian Leahy was already a well known and respected musician in his own right, and had been working at The Sound Shop in Drogheda. It was during Phil's regular visits to the shop that they struck up a friendship, which was to lead to Brian becoming the fourth group member.

They were soon in great demand, and the bookings rolled in. They took up where The Trolls left off, and were booked to play at many of their old venues. They were also booked by Delvin Rugby Club to play at their dances in The Village Hotel in Bettystown, and so began what turned out to be a sustained and very successful series of engagements. They continued with this line-up until 1977, when, due to family commitments, Shaun Black left the group.

Shaun's departure led to the return of the former Road Runner's drummer, Mick McLoughlin, but shortly afterwards, when Brian Leahy exited the group to take up a position with the already successful outfit known as the Village Folk, his departure was to spell the end of the road for The Lads. However, just as in several other instances, the end of this group quickly led to the formation of yet another.

With the recruitment of Rikki Martin as Brian's replacement, the new line-up consisted of the McLoughlin brothers Phil and Mick together with Timmy Regan and Rikki Martin. The new name for the group was "Again", and just like their predecessors, they were considered to be amongst the best of their era and enjoyed a great run of success. They continued playing until 1983 when, due to job commitments, Timmy had to leave the group. He was replaced by Rikki's brother Paul, and they continued with this line-up until late 1984, before finally deciding to bring down the curtain on a long and sustained run of successes.

Following the demise of the group, Rikki and Phil formed a great and enduring partnership, and although they now only make occasional appearances, they are still guaranteed a great reception.

I should also mention here that, as this section of the book contains quite a number of changes, not only in personnel but also in the group names, I have included a selection of photographs which I hope will be of assistance in this regard.

CHAPTER THIRTY SEVEN

PAT MOVES AROUND

Prior to his role in founding The Marksmen in 1969, lead guitarist Pat Moonan began his career as a guitarist at the age of thirteen, when he received tuition from Ollie Floody in Drogheda. Together with a few friends from his locality they formed a group known as Zounds which included Pat Moonan (rhythm guitar), Oliver Callaghan (lead guitar), Paddy Flanagan (bass guitar), Gerry Fahy (drums) and Michael Callaghan (vocalist). Pat also received further guitar lessons at The Sound Shop, Drogheda, where his tutor was none other than my good friend Eamonn Campbell, who later became a permanent member of The Dubliners.

Following the demise of The Marksmen, Pat became a member of The Cyril

Zounds:
Gerry Fahy , Oliver Callaghan, Pat Moonan, Michael Callaghan, Paddy Flanagan

Jolley Group, where he remained for several years. During the early 1980s he joined an already established group from Drumconrath Co. Meath known as Hamlet. The line-up of this group consisted of Pat (lead guitar), Brendan Clarke (rhythm guitar), Martin Callan (drums) and Seamie Walsh (vocalist).

Having enjoyed a very successful spell with Hamlet, Pat decided to team up with another already established three piece outfit known as The Blue Beats. The group consisted of Leo Larkin (rhythm guitar), Paddy Brady (bass guitar) and Vinnie Byrne (drums) and together with Pat on lead guitar, The Blue Beats proceeded as a four piece outfit. This group is of particular interest to me because, not only was Paddy Brady a former band mate of Pat during their Marksmen days, but as I have previously mentioned, both Leo Larkin and Vinnie Byrne shared a stage with Mickey Rooney and me during that infamous talent contest of the early 1970s.

During the latter half of the 1980s, Pat was involved in the formation of another new four piece outfit known as Ring-A-Ding, and the line-up consisted of Pat (lead guitar), Paddy Flanagan (rhythm guitar), Jodie Moonan (drums), and Seanie Neilon (vocalist).

In 1988 Pat parted company with Ring-A-Ding, and joined Unison, an already established four piece outfit which consisted of Leo Larkin (rhythm guitar), Tony Barrett (keyboards/trumpet), Johnny Barton (drums), and Anne Toner (vocalist). With Pat on lead guitar, they proceeded as a five piece outfit and continued their successful run for the next nine years.

In 1997 Pat again teamed up with Cyril Jolley, and together with Tommy Martin (drums/vocalist), this three piece outfit became known as The Beech Boys. They established a niche market for themselves when they embarked on a series of dances which became known as The Ballroom of Romance. This venture became very popular and attracted significant audiences wherever they performed.

Finally, with such a long and successful career behind him, Pat is not thinking of retirement any day soon, as he is currently playing with yet another outfit known as Bold as Brass. This latest line-up consists of Pat (lead guitar), Tony Barrett (trumpet), Eddie Barrett (rhythm guitar), Johnny Milne (trombone) and

Paddy Byrne (vocalist). The position of drummer with this group is very often alternated between both Gerry Fahy and Davy Curran.

****

Following the disbandment of The Chancellors Showband, our saxophone player Ernie McCarthy decided to take a break from the music scene and throughout the 1970s his performances were limited to just an occasional gig. However, when his old mates from his showband days in Longford decided on a 1980s reunion, he once again took to the stage. The band re-formed under their new name of The Black Dots, and as part of their revival they embarked on a tour of the Irish Clubs in London. In particular they were invited to play a series of gigs at The Admirals in Cricklewood. Throughout the 1980s they limited their performances to guest appearances at venues around their home town of Longford, but in 1990 they returned once again to London for a repeat of their 1980s tour. In 1994 Ernie joined a local outfit for a series of Ballroom of Romance gigs. They performed under the name of Heartbeat and were subsequently re-named Starlight. The original line-up included Ernie (tenor saxophone), David Lynch (piano), Joe Kierans (rhythm guitar), Eugene Smith (bass guitar), Jackie Reilly (trumpet), and Patsy Thornton (drums), and following some changes in personnel, the line-up for Starlight included Sean Donnelly (guitar), Johnny Milne (trombone) and Noel Mooney (drums).

Ernie McCarthy with the Hi Lows Showband.

Matt Monroe, John Leonard, Erroll Sweeney, Larry Carolan,
in the Drake Inn, Finglas, Dublin.

Cork Song Contest: Rose O'Brien & Harry O'Reilly (Author).

CHAPTER THIRTY EIGHT

CITY BOYS MOVE ON

Another casualty of the decline of the Showband phenomenon was The City Showband, and, as in so many other instances, this also led to the formation of several smaller groups. The first group to emerge from The City Showband became known as Red Mountain Wine, and the four piece outfit included Tom McCann (bass guitar), Dessie (Edger) Gray (vocals), Wally Murphy (guitar) and Mick Cullen (drums).

After several months together the group decided on a change of musical direction, and this change resulted in the formation of two entirely different groups. Wally Murphy formed his own ballad group which became known as Travelling John. This group went on to enjoy great and enduring success throughout the following decades. Travelling John's original line-up was a three piece outfit and included Wally (banjo), Roy Kierans (guitar) and Tommy Hodgins (guitar).

Meanwhile, Tom McCann was instrumental in the formation of a blues band which adopted the name of Bernard Jenkins. He was joined in this venture by former City Showband drummer Murrough O'Brien. The line-up for this five piece outfit included Tom (bass guitar), Murrough (drums), Mick O'Hagen (lead singer and harmonica), Liam Cunningham, (keyboards and lead guitar) and Kevin O'Brien (saxophone). This group continued performing throughout 1970 and for most of 1971 before taking the decision to disband.

Mick O'Hagan joined a Dublin based blues group known as Cromwell and Tom decided to team up with former band mates Dessie (Edger) Gray and Liam Cunningham, and together with Patsy Murphy (drums), they put together another four piece group known as Columbo.

Dermot O'Brien & The Clubmen:
Back: Timmy Regan, Eamonn Campbell, Derek McCormack
Front: Tony Barrett, Dermot O'Brien, Johnny Barton.

Dermot O'Brien & The Clubmen
Back: Dermot O'Brien, Jimmy Fitzpatrick
Front: Fintan Stanley, Pat Jackson, Johnny Barton, Paddy Farrell.

CHAPTER THIRTY NINE

JACKIE TURNS PRO

Included amongst a number of leading trumpet players to be featured in the earlier part of this book, is renowned musician Jack Reilly. With a considerable degree of assistance from Father Kevin Connolly and Tom Kerr, Jack was the driving force behind the foundation of The Lourdes Brass Band in Drogheda, and it was hardly a surprise when his son Jackie decided to follow in his father's footsteps.

Jackie began his career with The Drogheda Brass and Reed Band where he learned to play the cornet. Later during the mid-1960s, under his father's guidance, he took up trumpet playing, and went on to play with some of the top

The Arrows
with Jackie Reilly (front left)

outfits in the country. He began his career in the latter half of the 1960s with The Volunteers Showband whose line-up consisted of Dan Heery (keyboards), Paddy Traynor (tenor sax), Jackie Reilly (trumpet), Jodie Murray (guitar), Pat Fitzpatrick (bass guitar), Billy Browne (drums), and Sean Whearty (vocalist).

With the experience of playing with a successful showband under his belt, Jackie took the decision to exit The Volunteers and to move on. Shortly afterwards, when he accepted an invitation to join another already established outfit known as The Toronto Showband, he became part of a team which included two other local musicians, John Flood (guitar) and Kevin O'Brien (baritone sax). Following a spell with this outfit, Jackie took the decision to embark on a career as a full time professional musician.

He moved to Dublin where he successfully auditioned for the position of Trumpeter with a full time group known as Betty and The Teen Beats. After a year of playing gigs throughout Ireland, the Teen Beats accepted an offer to move their base to England. They also decided on a new name for the duration of their English tour, and they became known as Shades of Green.
During this period Jackie also got to follow in the footsteps of The Beatles, when his group played a series of gigs at The Top Ten Club in Hamburg.

On his return to Ireland, Jackie decided to move on, spending one year playing with The Lions Showband before accepting an offer to join The Arrows Showband. In 1975 when Dickie Rock took over the role as lead singer with this outfit, the band assumed the new name of Dickie's Band. Jackie subsequently secured a position with the Bill Ryan and Buckshot Showband, and he remained with this outfit for several more years. Finally in 1979, he decided to take things easy and he brought the curtain down on his career as a full time professional musician.

Following his retirement from the entertainment scene, Jackie decided to offer some much needed assistance to his father. He assumed a teaching role with The Lourdes Brass Band, where he later became its musical director.

CHAPTER FORTY
THE WESTERN MOVIES
MARIANNE FAITHFUL AND CHART HITS

El Companeros, a new band with a new sound, made its debut appearance on the local scene during the mid-1970s. Companeros was the title of a 1970 Spaghetti Western movie, and the theme music for the film was composed and performed by the world renowned composer Ennio Morricone. When choosing a name for his new band, veteran musician Willie Healy simply prefixed "El" to the film title and he adopted the film's music score as his band's signature tune.

El Companeros:
Tony Barrett, Stephen McCann, Bruce Moran, Johnny Milne.
Willie Healy, (missing from photograph : Tom McCann)

The Wicked Chicken:
Tommy Hodgins, Tom McCann, Patsy Murphy, David Montgomery,
Midge Tiernan.

In preparation for their official launch, the band commenced rehearsals in a room at The Sound Shop on the North Quay. The line-up of the new six piece outfit consisted of Willie (trumpet), Tony Barrett (trumpet), Johnny Milne (trombone), Tom McCann (bass guitar), Stephen McCann (keyboards) and Bruce Moran (drums). With such an array of experienced and respected musicians, the band was quickly up and running.

With a fresh sounding music style, their appearances were eagerly sought for reunions, weddings and social events generally and they invariably played to capacity audiences at such venues as The Fairways Hotel Dundalk, The Russell Arms Hotel, Navan, and The Windmill Hotel, Skerries. In addition, they played a series of regular gigs at The Star and Crescent Club in Drogheda. They generally played a lot of contemporary music at these gigs, but as their brass section was a significant element of the band's line-up, they successfully exploited this situation by including an amount of Tijuana Brass style music in their repertoire.

When Tony Barrett decided to move on, he was replaced on trumpet by Noel (Syd) Kierans. This was the only change in personnel to the line-up of the band during a successful innings which lasted for almost two years. The final curtain was brought down on El Companeros during the latter half of the 1970s, and following the dissolution of this outfit the individual members dispersed. Like true professionals, they continued to entertain for many more years and I will, no doubt, have more to say about them elsewhere.

Sometime after his exit from El Companeros, bass Guitarist Tom McCann teamed up with his pal Tommy Hodgins and, together with three more of their musician friends, they formed a new heavy metal outfit called The Wicked Chicken. Although this outfit only lasted for less than one year, they certainly made an impact on the local rock scene. They were featured at such venues as The Gem Lounge Bar on West Street Drogheda, and they secured a semi-resident spot at one of Dundalk's top rock venues The River Rooms. The line-up which remained unchanged throughout their successful run consisted of Tom McCann (bass guitar), Tommy Hodgins (rhythm guitar), David Montgomery (rhythm guitar) and Midge Tiernan (lead guitar).

****

As promised earlier, I will now take up the story of Paddy Kelly and Reunion, including an account of the group's lead guitarist Ben Corcoran.

Following the dissolution of the outfit known as Tracks, Ben Corcoran decided to pursue a career in music, and to this end he returned to college in 1973. During this period from 1973 to 1976, he continued to play music with various outfits. In addition, he played some session work, and in 1975 he secured a position as guitarist with The Gaiety Theatre Orchestra in Dublin. He had been playing with the orchestra for three months, when he was invited to join the already established and very successful group known as Reunion.

The line-up for this group consisted of Paddy Kelly (guitar/vocals), Peter Halpenny (bass guitar), Patsy Finnegan (drums) and Ben (lead guitar).

Reunion:
Patsy Finnegan, Peter Halpenny, Ben Corcoran, Paddy Kelly

Reunion had already secured a semi residency spot at The Fairways Hotel Dundalk, where they were booked to play on most Thursdays and Sundays. This arrangement continued for most of 1976, and part of 1977.

In May 1977, the group was approached by a promoter who wished to hire Reunion as the backing band for international singing star Marianne Faithful during her Irish tour. As Marianne's recording of Dreaming My Dreams was at number one in the charts, this was to be a promotional tour, and of course the group readily accepted the generous offer. Every concert was sold out and they were greeted by massive crowds at each venue. Meanwhile, whenever possible, the group continued to perform at The Fairways Hotel. Their appearances with Marianne attracted a lot of attention, and in September 1977 they became the only Irish group to make an appearance on I.T.V.'s top talent show New Faces. Paddy Kelly sang the Dr Hook hit "The Ballad of Lucy Jordan" on the show. The group's performance attracted the attention of dance promoters everywhere, and they quickly released a recording of another Dr Hook song entitled "Sing Me A Rainbow". They followed this up with a recording of Long John Baldry's "Let The Heartaches Begin". Both songs featured Paddy Kelly, and they reached number 2 and number 4 respectively in the Irish charts.

In the late 1970s, Reunion decided to form an eleven piece big band to perform a series of gigs as a Neil Diamond tribute band. However, during this period they continued with their regular group, and in order to avoid a clash of bookings, the gigs for each outfit were organised to run in tandem with each other. The line-up which augmented Reunion for the tribute gigs included Syd Kierans (trumpet), Frankie Smith (trumpet), Terry Smith (saxophone), Sean Byrne (saxophone), Johnny Milne (trombone), Danny Kierans (trombone) and Jimmy Walsh (keyboards). This Neil Diamond tribute band featured Paddy Kelly on vocals and was a great success. They were booked to perform at many of the prime cabaret venues nationally.

Reunion decided to call it a day in the early 1980s and Ben Corcoran retired from full time gigging. Ben had previously held a music teaching position at Balbriggan V.E.C., and in 1981 he secured a music teaching post at Drogheda V.E.C. He held this position until his retirement from teaching in 1986.

The Blue Beats
Leo Larkin, Vinnie Byrne, Pat Moonan, Brendan Reilly.

Barry & Marie Cluskey with Podger Reynolds.

CHAPTER FORTY ONE

MY LEISURELY STROLL THROUGH THE CABARET SCENE

Some months after the demise of The Chancellors Showband in late 1969, as previously mentioned, Jim Kierans of Jay Kay Promotions persuaded me to take on the role of lead guitarist with the resident group for The Boyne Valley Hotel's cabaret nights. My return to the stage in early 1970 was to last for a very long while, and this seems like the ideal place to include an account of my own subsequent career and the various outfits with which I've played. I am especially delighted to have the opportunity of introducing you to the many wonderful musicians I've had the pleasure of sharing many a stage with over the following decades.

The Boyne Valley cabaret group line-up featured Paddy Neary (accordion/piano) and Nicky Callan (trumpet and guitar) and I played lead guitar. A typical night at the cabaret consisted of a meal, followed by a floor show and a dance. Our group provided the music for dancing in addition to any support required by the visiting cabaret acts. These shows were very popular with the public and pre-booking of tables for most evenings became the norm. I played with this group for the duration of the cabaret season which lasted for most of 1970.

During my time at the Boyne Valley Hotel, I had been providing guitar lessons to a friend of mine called Leo Larkin. Leo's enthusiasm for the guitar was such that, in the space of a few short months, not only had he formed a three piece outfit, but he had also secured a resident spot for this group at McCrumlish's Lounge in Drogheda. On hearing that the cabaret nights were coming to an end, Leo invited me to join his outfit, and when he told me that the line-up included Mickey Rooney, my old pal from The Chancellors, I couldn't resist. The new four piece outfit consisted of Mickey Rooney (vocals), Leo Larkin (rhythm guitar), Vinny Byrne (drums). I assumed the role of lead guitarist.

In addition to our regular gigs at McCrumlishes, which included playing host to a certain talent contest, we were also very much in demand to play at various other venues throughout the region. In 1972, I accepted an offer to join the resident group at The Central Cabaret Lounge in Balbriggan, Co. Dublin, and following my decision to move on, Leo and the boys continued to perform for many years afterwards.

The Central Cabaret Lounge was already the prime entertainment venue in Balbriggan, and many of Ireland's leading cabaret entertainers were featured there on a weekly basis. The newly formed resident group was known as The Crystals and the line-up consisted of Jimmy Day (vocals and MC), Peter Flynn (keyboards), Mick Cullen (drums) and I played lead guitar.

Jimmy Day had been a leading member of The Cadets Showband, and his nightly performances with our outfit, coupled with those of the visiting cabaret stars, meant that every night at The Central was a full-house affair. Our drummer Mick Cullen had previously been a member of Drogheda based outfit Red Mountain Wine, and keyboard player Peter Flynn had been a member of the original resident group at The Central.

The Crystals continued with their successful run, and the line-up remained unchanged over the course of the next year. There was just one change in personnel during our time at The Central. In mid-1973 Jimmy Day decided to pursue a career as a cabaret act in his own right and another leading Dublin vocalist Gerry Murphy was chosen as his replacement. With Gerry as our new singer/MC, The Crystals continued with their successful run at The Central in Balbriggan until mid-1974 when the decision was taken to move on.

Gerry Murphy returned to performing at venues around his native Dublin and Mick Cullen took the decision to take a break from playing. However, during our time at The Central, my old mate Paddy Toner had been acting as a replacement drummer for Mick Cullen, and when Peter Flynn and I decided to carry on gigging, we asked Paddy to accompany us in a new three piece outfit also known as The Crystals.

Some months afterwards whilst playing at a gig in The Big Tree Lounge Bar in Clogherhead, we were approached by the management of The Beach Tavern Cabaret Lounge in Balbriggan who had been there to hear our group. They had replaced The Central Lounge as Balbriggan's main cabaret venue, and as we were already very popular with The Balbriggan public, they offered us the position of resident backing group at their venue. We readily accepted, and so began a further eighteen months of playing to capacity audiences and accompanying many of Ireland's top cabaret acts. When we finally brought the curtain down on our time at Balbriggan, our keyboard player Peter Flynn decided to exit the group and Paddy Toner and I decided to form a new Drogheda based group.

In late 1975 we set about forming a new four piece outfit known as Unit Four and the line-up consisted of Raymond Green (rhythm guitar), Tony Cassidy (bass guitar), Paddy Toner (drums) and I played lead guitar. Tony and Raymond were two of my former pals from our garage-playing days, and in addition Tony, Paddy and I were former members of The Chancellors Showband. Following a few weeks of rehearsals, we played our first gigs in early 1976 and the new combination proved to be an instant success. We invariably drew large audiences and we were especially popular at The Blues Club, Drogheda where we played on a weekly basis. The weather was wonderful during the summer season of 1976, and I still have fond memories of that year as we played to capacity audiences at Sharkey's Lounge in Clogherhead.

The group only lasted for little more than one year and, at the beginning of 1977 when we brought the curtain down on Unit Four, Raymond Greene embarked on a solo career while Tony Cassidy (Bass Guitar) together with Johnny Bolger (Rhythm Guitar) and Terry Sands (Drums) formed an excellent three piece outfit known as Tailormade. I continued to play with various other groups, and in particular I recall playing at quite a number of gigs with John

The Ravens:
Liam Carter, Paddy Toner (drums) Harry O'Reilly
(in the Grove Hotel , Dunleer 1980)

Leonard and his band, at the Drake Inn in Dublin. Meanwhile Paddy Toner teamed up with Liam Carter and The Ravens, and this seems like the ideal place to include a report on yet another of Drogheda's leading outfits known as The Ravens.

During the mid 1950s Liam Carter began his musical career with The Drogheda Brass and Reed Band and under the tuition of the band's musical director Jimmy Nash, he learned to play the cornet. At the beginning of the 1970s his brother Sean was already a member of the popular Dunleer based group known as The Premier Trio and Liam was keen to follow in his brother's footsteps.

Liam and his friends, Fintan Keegan (guitar) and Oliver Dyas (drums), had been considering for some time about forming their own musical group, and in early 1972 they took the decision to put their plans into practice. They began by hiring some P.A. equipment from Tommy Leddy's Sound shop, and they secured the use of a room at The Grange Inn at Grangebellew, Co. Louth for their rehearsals. Initially, Liam did not play any instrument, but some time afterwards he learned to play guitar. The group undertook a period of intense rehearsals during which time they built up a significant repertoire. They also chose The Ravens as their group name. Meanwhile, the management of The Grange had been monitoring the group's progress and they must have been sufficiently impressed because they offered them the opportunity to play their first gig at The Grange Inn.

Following a successful launch, the group began receiving bookings from a range of venues throughout the locality. The Ravens were set fair for a long and sustained run of successes which would continue right up to the mid-1980s. Inevitably there were several changes in personnel over the years, but the one constant throughout was Liam Carter, the founding member who remained with the various combinations of this group throughout its existence.

In 1973 when Oliver Dyas decided to exit The Ravens, he was replaced on drums by Tom (Twiggy) Byrne. This line-up continued for the next eighteen months until mid 1975. When Fintan Keegan decided to move on, he was replaced on guitar/vocals by Shaun Reynolds, and shortly afterwards when Twiggy Byrne also took the decision to move on, he was replaced on drums by Tony (Stony) Burke. The new three piece line-up of Liam Carter, Shaun Reynolds, and Stony Burke continued unaltered from 1975 through to 1977.

Some further changes in personnel took place following the departure of Stony Burke in mid-1977. Paddy Toner was recruited as the group's new drummer, and some months afterwards, when Shaun Reynolds took the decision to exit the group, I accepted an offer from Liam and Paddy to join The Ravens.

The line-up of Liam Carter (bass guitar), Harry O'Reilly (guitar) and Paddy Toner (drums) that took to the stage in early 1978 was set fair for a long and sustained successful run. We were extremely popular with audiences throughout the region and enjoyed an uninterrupted run of success which lasted for almost eight years. When the final curtain was drawn in early 1986, it brought to an end the longest and also the final line-up to appear under the

Swiss Trio:
Rose O'Brien, Aidan Brodigan, Harry O'Reilly,
photo Andy Spearman.

banner of The Ravens.

Following the dissolution of The Ravens, Liam Carter decided to continue his musical career as a solo performer, and both Paddy Toner and I decided to take a lengthy break from gigging. Although Paddy's break turned out to be a permanent one, my break came to an end during late 1989 when I was persuaded to resume gigging, and it is with a report on my final outfit which became known as The Swiss Trio, that I will bring the curtain down on my own career in music.

Aidan Brodigan, a keyboard player and former school-mate of mine, had been performing as a solo artist for several years, and when he approached me with a view to forming a new musical group, I agreed to accompany him on some of his gigs where we performed as a two-piece outfit. On completion of these initial gigs, I persuaded Aidan that our best option for success would be to proceed as a three-piece. He immediately suggested that we should consider featuring a female vocalist in our new line-up. To this end we approached Tullyallen based singer Rose O'Brien, and luckily she was available at that time to join our new outfit.

Rose was widely acknowledged as a great vocalist with a great all-round stage personality, and had already built up a reputation both as a solo performer and as member of several other leading outfits such as The Mountaineers. Although Rose had a preference for singing Country and Western style songs, and in particular her renditions of many of Patsy Cline's songs were nightly show-stoppers, nevertheless her all-round singing ability endeared her to fans everywhere.

Aidan Brodigan's suggestion that the group should be known as The Swiss Trio was accepted, and we launched our new three-piece outfit at The Drogheda United F.C. function rooms on Windmill Road on New Year's Eve 1989. The night was a resounding success and the group was well and truly on its way. During the next few years, we performed at most of the venues throughout the region where we built up a significant fan base. In particular we secured a regular slot at The Sail Inn, Clogherhead, where our series of summertime gigs were very often sell-out affairs.

During the period 1993 to 1997, I wrote a number of songs, and with the assistance of Rose and her great voice, I had them recorded for entry into several of the major song contests nationally. The format for these competitions requires the songwriter to supply a recorded version of the song together with a copy of the lyrics and to submit them for analysis by a panel of adjudicators. It was a great honour to have some of my songs selected for inclusion in the finals of such contests as The Cavan International Song contest, The Bantry song Contest, Glinsk Song Contest, and the Cork International Peace Song Contest.

Throughout the first couple of stages of this book, the focus has been on the Drogheda based bands and musicians who became household names during the period 1940 through to 1970. Post 1970 I have maintained the focus on the individual musicians from that earlier period, together with a less comprehensive look at the outfits and the subsequent generation of musicians with which they became associated. However, the production of the necessary backing tracks and the completion of the professional recordings for the various Song Contests, presented me with the opportunity to work with two of the current generation's top musicians, David Leddy and Gerry Simpson. Prior to each recording session, using his considerable musical skills, David produced some great arrangements for me, and afterwards, Gerry produced some superb and overall polished recordings of my songs in his recording studio. With musicians of this calibre, there is little doubt that Drogheda's great musical tradition is currently in safe hands and prospects for the future look very bright indeed.

Finally, The Swiss Trio continued with their successful run for several more years, and with the original combination still intact, the final curtain was drawn on New Year's Eve, 1996.

CHAPTER FORTY TWO

THE FULL CIRCLE

I began my review of Drogheda's finest bands with a report on The Flying Carlton Orchestra, and it seems most appropriate that the concluding review should be of The Carlton All Stars, a six piece outfit formed almost fifty years later, which still featured three members of the original orchestra in its line-up. What better way to demonstrate the continuity and well-being of Drogheda's music and its musicians.

During the late 1980s, local musicians, Willie Healy (trumpet), Ramie Smith (drums) and Johnnie Milne (trombone), persuaded three of their former colleagues, Syd Kierans (trumpet), Brendan Munster (tenor sax)

The Carlton All Stars:
Brendan Munster, Ramie Smith, Sean Donnelly,
Syd Kierans, Willie Healy, Johnny Milne.

The Pantomime Orchestra:
Christy Smith, Kevin O'Brien, Danny Kierans, Maurice Smith, John (Twick) Donnelly, David Leddy, Brendan Munster,
Front: Conductor : Jimmy Nash

The Brass & Reed Band 1943

and Sean Donnelly (guitar), to put together a new outfit to be known as The Carlton All Stars. With all six musicians already veterans of the Drogheda dance scene and with Willie, Syd, and Brendan, three former members of The Flying Carlton in their ranks, the name for their new band was a fairly obvious one. With such a collection of fine musicians in the line-up, The Carlton All Stars quickly established themselves, and with a distinctive sound and unique style of music, their performances were acclaimed throughout the region.

Over the course of several generations, the musical careers of many of Drogheda's finest musicians began with the Drogheda Brass and Reed Band, and in keeping with that organisation's long tradition, quite a few of them returned there to devote much of their valuable time in passing on their acquired skill to each subsequent generation of new recruits. Not only does The Carlton All Stars represent the continuity of Drogheda's dance bands, but they also have very strong links to The Drogheda Brass and Reed Band in this respect.

Louis Smith

CHAPTER FORTY THREE

THE BRASS BAND CONNECTION

When referring to the increased demand for dance bands during the 1940s/1950s, I suggested that the seemingly endless supply of new bands emerging from Drogheda during this period was mainly due to the wonderful musical training establishments already available in the town. I am delighted to be able to pay tribute not only to these organisations and the members who worked tirelessly within them, but also to some of the individual music teachers who were so generous in passing on their skills and techniques to each new generation of would-be musicians.

Without doubt, The Drogheda Brass and Reed Band stands out like a beacon when referring to the musical heritage of the town, and the contents of an entire book would be required to fully do justice to that organisation. I am aware that The Drogheda Brass and Reed Band is currently known as The Drogheda Brass Band, but for most of the period under review in this book, the use of the former name is most likely the appropriate one. However, for information purposes only, I have put together a brief history of its origin.

When it was first formed in 1886, The Drogheda Brass and Reed Band became known as The Colonel Leonard Fife and Drum Band. Colonel Leonard hailed from Monleek near Tullyallen, where in 1887 the local Tullyallen G.A.A. Club also assumed the name of The Colonel Leonard Football Club. He emigrated to America where he joined the 69th New York Regiment of The Union Army and rose to the rank of Colonel. He subsequently returned to Ireland and became a leader in the Fenian rising of 1867. He managed to evade capture and spent his remaining years in Drogheda until his death in 1873. He is buried in Monknewtown cemetery near Slane, Co. Meath.

On the disbandment of the 5th Leinster Regiment, which had been stationed in Millmount Barracks in 1906, the regiment's musical instruments became available and were purchased by the Drogheda band for the reputed sum of £5.00. The Band was renamed the Drogheda Brass and Reed Band, and they later moved from their original location on Mill Lane to the band rooms on Georges Street. Finally in 1964 the band became an all-brass combination, and the title was subsequently changed to that of The Drogheda Brass Band.

The success or otherwise, of any organisation is usually dependent on the drive, ambition, and skill of its members, and no doubt over the course of its history, there were numerous such individuals in charge at The Drogheda Brass and Reed Band. When I enrolled at the Georges Street band rooms in 1953, the musical director was Jimmy Nash, and without doubt he possessed all of these qualities in abundance. At that time, Jimmy was ably assisted by numerous other equally committed members, such as Jack Reilly who was later credited with the formation of The Lourdes Brass Band, and Syd Kierans who was instrumental in the formation of The Dunleer Brass Band, and who also played a major role in the continuation and enhancement of both The Ardee and Kingscourt Brass and Reed Bands.

To further demonstrate the continuity and well-being of Drogheda's music and the generosity of its musicians in passing on their acquired skills, I have included an account of their involvement with the Kingscourt Brass and Reed Band.

In an effort to restore his town's ailing brass band to its former glory, Andy Reilly, a native of Kingscourt and a cornet player with the band, turned to his old friend Jimmy Nash of Drogheda's Brass and Reed Band. Jimmy's response was to encourage three of his fellow Drogheda musicians, Syd Kierans, Brendan Munster, and Ramie Smith, to assist him with the task. This team of top class musicians made the weekly journey to Kingscourt where they were enthusiastically welcomed by the local community. With a combination of superb tuition, new instruments, and new band uniforms, the outcome was almost inevitable.

This excellent band was not only invited to play at venues here at home, but also performed at several international venues including London and Berne Switzerland. In addition, they were invited to represent Cavan at the New York St Patrick's Day parades of 1997 and 2004. The itinerary for these events was organised by the band's secretary Jim O'Reilly. The band was widely acclaimed for their performance, as they proudly marched up 5th Avenue during their participation in the parades. They also received a number of invitations to display their talents at several of New York's famous venues.

In conclusion, the committee of The Kingscourt Brass and Reed Band showed their appreciation for the Drogheda musicians contribution to their band, by extending an invitation to accompany them on an expenses paid eight-day trip for the band's 2004 visit to New York, where in addition to participating in the St Patricks Day Parade, the band performed at New York's St. Patricks Cathedral, and followed this with a performance on the 85th floor of The Empire State Building.

Quite apart from Drogheda's recognised musical training establishments such as The Drogheda Brass Band, The Lourdes Brass Band, The Crilly School of Music, and The Sound Shop Music School, the tradition of this town's individual musicians, who for so many years have willingly passed on their acquired skills to future musicians, is still alive and well today, and hopefully will continue for many years to come. With so many outstanding music teachers to choose from, I have decided to complete this section by singling out four individuals with whom I have been personally acquainted over the years, and who have devoted so much of their valuable time to passing on their musical skills to future generations.

The man who first introduced me to music following my enrolment at the Drogheda band rooms when I was seven years of age, was Brass Band Supremo Jimmy Nash, about whom so much has already been written; former English Champion Accordionist and distinguished band leader Cyril Jolley, who became my accordion teacher when I was nine years of age; Louis Smith

Willie Healy's Lourdes Church Choir 1959

who was an inspiration to me and many other young musicians who were lucky enough to share a stage with him; Willie Healy who made his debut as a trumpet player with The Kay Martin Orchestra in 1948, and who went on to feature in many of Ireland's leading bands over the following decades.

Much of Willie's career in show business is well documented. However, there is another aspect which is not so well known, and in keeping with the current theme, I feel I must include the following piece of information. In the wake of a serious illness in 1955, Willie found himself unable to play his trumpet so he embarked on a period of piano tuition at The Crilly School of music. Sometime afterwards in 1958, he was approached by Father Connolly regarding the formation of a choir in preparation for the opening of the new Our Lady of Lourdes Church. Armed with his newly acquired piano playing skills, Willie set about recruiting and training his choir for their debut church performance. Following a successful launch of his new choir, Willie continued as church organist and choir master for the next few years, before once again returning to the stage.

Even before I had reached the halfway stage of writing this book, with new bands and musicians emerging on an almost daily basis in this vibrant musical town, I came to realise that another book or sequel to this one would be almost inevitable. As I endeavoured to deal comprehensively with the period from the 1940s through to the 1970s, a crossover between the earlier generation of bands and musicians and those of the ensuing generations was also inevitable. There are a whole host of local bands and musicians who are currently household names and whose talents are acknowledged throughout the country and beyond. Many of them have already been briefly mentioned in the course of this book, but unfortunately I felt constrained and unable to give them due prominence. However I have no doubt they will feature prominently in any future such publication.

During the course of my research, I was greeted by so many of my old friends and I must express my gratitude for the hospitality which was extended to me on every occasion. I am deeply indebted to all of those individuals who were so helpful in supplying me with the information and the photographs which I sought, and which were so necessary for the successful completion of the book. I recall a conversation I shared with renowned vocalist Timmy Regan, on one such visit to his home. As I sat busily taking notes, Timmy enquired if I found the amount of effort required for the research and preparation of the book to be both troublesome and time-consuming, but before I could offer a suitable comment, he added "I'd say it must be a labour of love for you". I agreed with Timmy at that time, and now that the work is complete, I can't think of a better way to bring the curtain down on this book than to add that it has indeed been a labour of love for me.

Drogheda Brass & Reed Band:
50 Years on – Award Ceremony

Peadar Smith

Tony Cassidy, Roy McCormack, Harry O'Reilly (author),
three guitarists at The Shadows Concert, Dublin.

Shaun Reynolds, Francie Flanagan, David Leddy,
at the TLT, Drogheda.

Vinnie Byrne

Pa Carter (guitar) with the Comet Tones Showband

Pantomime Orchestra
John (Twick) Donnelly, Sean Byrne, Johnny Barton, Kevin O'Brien, Peter Milne, Terry Smith, Ben Mullen, Brendan Munster, Louis Smith, Syd Kierans, Raphael Kierans, Danny Kierans, Willie Healy.

Jim Byrne (drums) Johnny Murray (accordion) Pa Carter (guitar)

The Gate Cinema Orchestra

Eileen Matthews with the Astoria Orchestra

Astoria - at the Whitworth Hall:
Danny Kierans, George Reilly (drums) Sean Donnelly, Sean Kierans, Jack Cluskey,
Brendan Munster, Dominic McManus.

INDEX

OF NAMES

Carton, Jim

Carton, Patsy

Cash, Johnny

Cassidy, Brian

Cassidy, Frank

Cassidy, Tony

Chesser, Don

Clarke, Brendan

Cline, Patsy

Cluskey, Barry

Cluskey, Jack

Condon, Billy

Conlon, Mo

Connolly, Billy

Connolly, Fr. Kevin

Connor, Benny

Connor, Paddy

Cooper, John Joe

Corcoran, Ben

Corcoran, Jimmy

Corrigan, Niall

Coyle, Jim

Coyle, Paddy

Crean, Brendan

Crosby, Bing

Cudden, Frankie

Cullen, Mick

Cunningham, Liam

Curran, Davy

Daniels, Charlie

Daniels, Roly

Dankworth, Johnny

Day, Jimmy

Delaney, John

Delany, Jim (Jazz)

Diamond, Neil

Doherty, Mick

Donnelly, Dave

Donnelly, John

Donnelly, John (Twick)

Donnelly, Peter

Donnelly, Sean

Donnelly, Tommy (Bongo)

Doonican, Val

Dowd, Patsy

Downey, Maurice

Doyle, Kenny

Doyle, Larry

Doyle, Marie (Martin)

Duff, Mary

Dyas, Oliver

Eager, David

English, Jimmy

Fagan, Derek

Fagan, Jimmy

Fagan, Lily

Fahy, Gerry

Faithful, Marianne

Farrell, Gerry

Farrell, Larry

Farrell, Paddy (Drogheda)

Farrell, Paddy (Laytown)

Fay, Dessie (Skinner)

Finglas, Brian

Finglas, Dermot

Finglas, Tom

Finnegan, Pat

Finnegan, Patsy

Fitzpatrick, Jimmy

Fitzpatrick, Pat

Flanagan, Paddy

Flood, Ita

Flood, John

Floody, Ollie

Floody, Patsy

Flynn, Peter

Flynn, Willie

Fox, Pat

Gallagher, Bridie

Gallagher, Rory

Gibney, Dave

Gloria

Godfrey, Joan

Gogarty, John

Goodman, Benny

Gordon, Ben

Goring, Brendan (Red)

Gough, Aidan

Gough, Mrs

Grace, Brendan

Gray, Dessie (Edger)

Green, Hughie

Green, Raymond

Grey Jimmy

Haley, Bill

Halpenny, Peter

Halpin, Joe

Hand (O'Reilly), Susan

Hand, Jim

Hand, Michael (Mickser)

Hanratty, John

Harte, Paul

Healy, Tommy (Bubbles)

Healy, Willie

Heeney, Paddy

Heeney, Terry

Heery, Dan

Hegarty, Dermot

Henry, Mike (Magic)

Herman, Buddy

Hilton, Kevin

Hodgins, Tommy

Hoey, Brian

Hopkins, Billy

Hopkins, Des

Hughes, Gerry

Hughes, Tim

Hurley, Red

Jackson, Pat

John, (Glenfarne)

Jolley, Cyril

Jordan, Neil

Kavanagh, Jim

Kearns, Paddy

Keegan, Fintan

Kelly, David

Kelly, Gerry

Kelly, John

Kelly, Matt

Kelly, Paddy

Kelly, Sandy (Duskey)

Kennedy, Ronnie

Kenny, Tony

Kerley, Dermot

Kerr, Tom

Kierans, Danny

Kierans, Eugene (Oodie)

Kierans, Eva

Kierans, Jim

Kierans, Joe

Kierans, Neil

Kierans, Noel (Syd)

Kierans, Paddy

Kierans, Roy

Kierans, Sean

Kierans, Tony

King, Liz

Kingston, Noel

Krantz, Rosen

Larkin, Leo

Leahy, Brian

Leddy, Tommy

Leddy, David,

Ledingham, Jon

Leech, Joe

Leech, Pat

Leonard, Colonel Patrick

Leonard, John

Lewis, Jerry Lee

Little Richard

Lloyd, Reggie

Logan, Johnny

Lynch, Owen

Lynch, Ralph

Lynch, Brian

Lynch, David

Lynch, Joe

Lynch, Maurice

Lynch, Owen

Magee, Charlie

Margo

Martin, Francie

Martin, Harry

Martin, Jervis

Martin, John

Martin, Kevin

Martin, Paul

Martin, Rikki

Martin, Tommy

Martin, Tony

Matthews, Eileen,

Matthews, Tommy

McCann, Joe

McCann, Paddy (Hardship)

McCann, Stephen

McCann, Stephen Jnr.

McCann, Tom

McCarthy, Ernie

McCarthy, Eugene

McConnon, Brendan

McCormack, Derek

McCormack, Roy

McCormack, Hugh

McCormack, Marie (Martin)

McCormack, Nan

McCormack, Tony

McDaniels, Maisie

McDonnell, Pal

McDonnell, Pat

McDonnell, Stephen

McDonnell, Tommy

McEnteggart, Charlie

McEvoy, Tommy

McGee, Paul

McGonigle, Mary

McGoona, Mattie

McGowan, Mick

McGuffin, Bob

McKenny, Phyllis

McLoughlin, Francie

Mcloughlin, Joe

McLoughlin, Mick

McLoughlin, Phil (Birch)

McManus, Dessie

McManus, Dominic

Melley, George

Milne, Johnny

Monaghan, Johnny

Montgomery, David

Moonan, Ben

Moonan, Jodie

Moonan, Pat

Moonan, Tommy

Mooney, Noel

Mooney, Noel (Boots)

Mooney, P.J

Moore, Butch

Moore, John

Moore, Maisie

Moran, Bruce

Morgan, Martin

Moroney, Larry

Morricone, Ennio

Mountcharles, Lady Eileen

Mullen, Ben

Mullen, Oliver

Mulroy, Gerry

Munster, Brendan

Munster, Mary

Munster, Mickey

Murphy, Bobby

Murphy, Damien

Murphy, Gerry

Murphy, Martin

Murphy, Mickey

Murphy, Patsy

Murphy, Wally

Murray, Jodie

Nash, Jimmy

Nealon, Seanie

Neary, Paddy

Newman, Jimmy

O'Brien, Dermot

O'Brien, Dougie

O'Brien, Kevin

O'Brien, Murragh

O'Brien, Rose

O'Brien, Sean

O'Callaghan, Deirdre

O'Donnell, Daniel

O'Dowd, Colin

O'Hagan, Mick

O'Kane, Paul (Cisco)

O'Loughlin, Denis

O'Neill, Phil

O'Reilly, Gaye

O'Reilly, Irene

O'Reilly, Jack

O'Reilly, Jim

O'Reilly, John

O'Reilly, Kenneth

O'Reilly, Liam

O'Reilly, Mary

O'Reilly, Paddy

O'Rourke, Denis

Orbison, Roy

Owens, Jessie

Phillips, Carl

Potter, Maureen

Quinn, Frank

Quinn, Martin

Raphael, Kierans

Regan, Timmy

Reilly, Andy

Reilly, George

Reilly, Jack

Reilly, Jackie

Reilly, Paddy

Reilly, Tom

Reily, Paddy

Reynolds, Bill

Reynolds, Jim

Reynolds, Paddy (Podger)

Reynolds, Shaun

Roche, Hal

Rock, Dickie

Roger, Jackie

Rogers, Val

Rooney, Mickey

Russell, Bobby

Ryan, Bill

Sands, Terry

Saurin, Bernie

Saurin, Gerry

Saurin, John

Shand, Jimmy

Shields, Billy

Shine, Brendan

Simpson, Gerry

Simpson, Spyder

Sinnott, Tom

Skelly, Terry

Slane, Viscount

Smith Ramie

Smith, Christy

Smith, Benny

Smith, Des

Smith, Eugene

Smith, Fr. Nick

Smith, Frankie

Smith, Joe

Smith, Larry

Smith, Louis

Smith, Maisie

Smith, Mary Anne
(The Nurse)

Smith, Peadar

Smith, Terry

Snow, Hank

Somers, John

Somers, Leontia

Spears, Billy Jo

Stanley, Fintan

Stewart, Louis

Sullivan, Tom

Sweeney, Erroll

Sweeney, Ian

Sweeney, Paddy

Taylor, Clarrie

Taylor, Robin

Thompson, Declan

Thornton, Patsy

Tiernan, Midge

Tinsley, Oliver

Toner, Anne

Toner, Paddy

Traynor, Gerry (Oscar)

Traynor, Mickey

Traynor, Paddy

Trench, Brian

Tynan, Rose

Victory, Maurice

Victory, Tommy

Wall, Mickey

Walpole, Jimmy

Walsh, Jimmy

Walsh, Seamus

Walsh, Tony

Walsh, Willie

Watters, Jimmy

Weldon, Martin

Whearty, Richard (Richie)

Whearty, Sean

White Patsy

White, Mrs.

White, Solomon (Solly)

White, Dominic (Dom)

White, Jim (Jemser)

White, Paddy

Wickham, Gerry

Woods, John

Wynne, Tony

The Louis Smith Big Band:
Back: Mike Jones, Eddie Barrett, Syd Kierans, Danny Kierans, Peter Milne, John (Twick) Donnelly, Louis Smith, Owen Lynch.
Front: Kevin O'Brien, Terry Heeney, Terry Smith, Ben Mullen, Jimmy Clynch.